Contents

AF192050

The
Bloody Husband
and
other weird stories

Magnus Viita

Publisher: BoD – Books on Demand, Helsinki, Finland

Manufacturer: BoD – Books on Demand, Norderstedt, Germany

ISBN: 978-952-80-8248-4

The Bloody Husband

"For it is the blood that maketh an atonement for the soul."
(Leviticus 17:11)

1.
July 15th

It was ten years since the events of that night. Nobody had visited the cabin ever since then. The real estate agent also quit renting the place and finally he forgot about it. However, suddenly – about a week ago – one married couple was asking for a peaceful place for vacation. Since all the available cabins were already taken, the agent had to go through his old archives. From these he found the papers of one luxury cabin, and since no other place was availabe, the agent was consent to rent it. The couple was delighted to have the kind of place they were looking for. The agent did mention about the distant location of the cabin, but it didn't reduce their enthusiasm – in fact quite the opposite.

This couple was formed by a man named Steven and his wife Caroline. Back in the day they had met at the graduation celebration of their hometown university. It was then Steven – a master of science – met his wife-to-be Caroline – a medical doctor. After noticing how much they had in common, they started dating. Their relationship progressed rapidly and finally reached its climax when Steven and Caroline got married at the local church. Now it was two years since then. This year the couple decided to spend their summer vacation at some peaceful place on the countryside – they'd had enough of their restless urban life. Steven and Caroline did check through many places from different agents, but none of those was really suitable for the couple. Finally, after they contacted the best agent of their city, they were succesful: a beautiful, large, oldfashioned cabin was found at the northern shore of a lake – far away from all disturbance. Steven and Caroline rented the cabin right away and then started to prepare for their dreamy vacation. It was today at about 8.15 a.m. when the couple began their road trip to the cabin. The path was quite complicated: because of this the car was often sidetracked and the couple had to ask instructions from the locals.

Finally – at about 5.40 p.m. – they arrived to the yard of their cabin. Steven stayed on the outside and started unpacking the car, Caroline on the other hand decided to take a look at the inside of the place. Very carefully she opened the creaking door and stepped inside. First she took off her sandals and then started walking barefoot on the wooden floor. Caroline was at the main hall of the cabin. It was decorated with embroidered carpets, colorful paintings and also with a soft antique sofa – located on the left side of the hall. Opposite this sofa was a cabinet full of old books – there was also a color TV on one of the shelves. After seeing all this Caroline thought they had made a good decision and would get worthy compensation for their money. It was then her eyesight met the wall opposite the hall door. There was an old, mechanical clock on this wall. The clock itself was in no way special – just a typical, oldfashioned clock. But the clock had stopped and its hands were excatly at 9.10. Caroline knew the time by looking at her wristwatch – it was already 5.44

p.m. – so she decided to wind up the clock. She stepped in front of the clock, found the winding key on top of it, put the key in the face of the clock and started to turn it. However, after she had turned the key more than enough, the clock still didn't start ticking. She then decided the clock was broken and let it be.

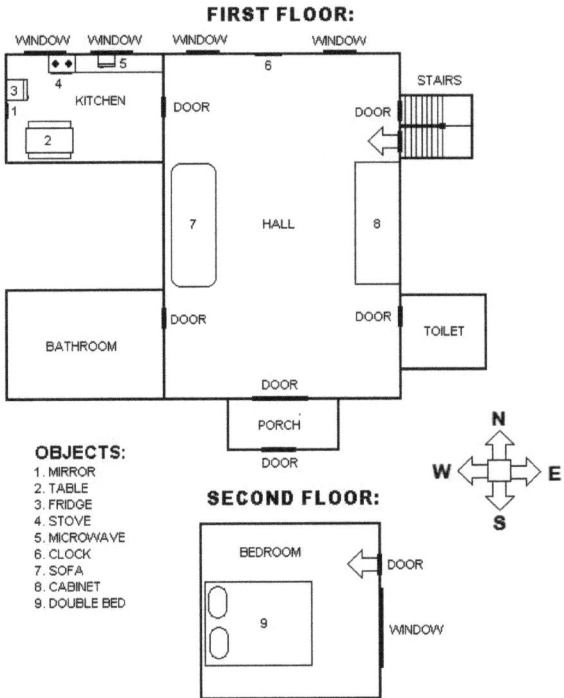

The Floor Plan of the Cabin.

Caroline went on checking the cabin further. She noticed two doors on the both sides of the sofa – left and right. The left one led to the bathroom and the right one to the kitchen with the dining space. Then she noticed yet another door on the right side of the cabinet, which led to the toilet. After noticing this she started to wonder where the bedroom was. This concern was soon gone after Caroline noticed there was still more space to explore: there was one more door on the left side of the cabinet. After opening it she found a staircase leading up to the second floor. She decided to check it out. The staircase was shaped like a spiral and the stairs gave a nasty creeping sound while she was going upstairs.

When Caroline reached the second floor door and opened it, she found what she was looking for – a good-sized bedroom with a double bed facing the door. There was a large window on the right side of the door. Caroline found this very pleasant since there was going to be a lunar eclipse after a couple of days – at 4.10 a.m. Now she and Steven would be able to watch it straight from the bed. Everything seemed to be in order in the bedroom. There was just one strange detail puzzling Caroline: the left mattress of the double bed was laying on the floor – at the lower end of the bed, on the lower left corner. At the leftmost corner of the mattress – from her point of view – there was a relatively large hole. She then thought it wouldn't be a problem since they had brought their very own bedsheets. Suddenly she heard a crashing sound coming from downstairs and was greatly startled – and was relieved after hearing Steven yelling and cursing: he was bringing in their suitcases and one of them had fallen on his right foot. Caroline wanted to do her own share of the chores. First she decided to lift the mattress back on the bed. She went barefoot on the wooden floor and stepped right next to the mattress.

In an instant she felt burning pain on the bottom of her right foot. The pain was so great she let out an ear-piercing cry and sat quickly on the mattress. Caroline looked at her right foot and saw on its bottom a wound – a deep, long cut from which blood was flowing as a straight line. Steven heard his wife screaming, appeared soon at the door and was shocked for the sight: his beloved was bleeding from her right foot to the mattress! The blood ran along the mattress and was flowing inside it through the hole on its corner.

Caroline was in great pain and asked her husband to go downstairs to get something for binding the wound. Right after that Steven went quickly down the staircase. Even though she was in pain on the foot, it didn't stop her from wondering what was the cause of this accident. Then her eyes met a pair of bloody scissors lying on the floor next to the mattess. She thought these were dropped accidentaly by one of the previous tenants, and therefore she had stepped on them – this had to be the cause. At the same moment Steven returned to the room with some tissue paper, disinfectant and linen cloth for binding. He went to his wife and started pressing the wound in order to stop the bleeding. He then rinsed the wound and bound it carefully. After this he also had time to wonder what had caused this. Silently she answered by pointing out the scissors on the floor. Steven picked up the bloody item and went again dowstairs to get something to clean up the bloody mattress. Caroline laid herself on the right-side mattress of the bed and was waiting the pain to leave. She closed her eyes.

Half a minute passed in perfect silence. But after that Caroline suddenly heard a weird sound: it was coming from the direction of the bloody mattress and sounded as if someone had slurped water from a glass! This sound made cold ripples run along her spine, because she saw no-one in the room. She didn't dare to move for fear to look under the bed. She was unable to imagine what was making the sound. Caroline was about to scream when the sound suddenly stopped. At the moment Steven came back upstairs. He was carrying the scissors that were cleaned of blood, a bottle of cleaner and a scrub-brush. When the wife saw her husband she leaped off the bed, embraced him and then told about the creepy sound she had heard.

Caroline and Steven both turned their eyes toward the mattress lying on the floor. What they next saw was incomprehensible: all of the blood on the mattress was gone − every single drop of it! Just a moment ago there had been blood all over the mattress, but now it had disappeared. There wasn't even any trace on the mattress. Caroline told she had done absolutely nothing. However, Steven couldn't believe her since blood doesn't just vanish all on its own. In any case they kept on preparing their vacation for the rest of the day. At first Steven took the groceries to the kitchen fridge while Caroline got the bedsheets from the car and took them to the bedroom upstairs. Then she lifted the left mattress back to the bed and spread new, clean sheets on both mattresses. Even though there was a hole on the left one it wouldn't be a problem since the sheets were nice and clean. After that the couple cleaned the cabin of dust and all other little somethings which had gathered during the years. Finally − when the day was turning towards the evening − they moved the night stand from the bed to the next of the window. Then they took the TV from downstairs and laid it on the night stand for watching. When the digital watch they had brought was displaying the time 9.35 p.m. they decided to go to sleep. Since their vacation would really start tomorrow it was necessary to get sufficient rest. Steven fell asleep quite soon, but Caroline stayed awake. She was still frightened by the vanishing of the blood from the mattress she was now lying on. She was even more scared by the slurping sound which came at the same moment – as if the mattress itself had drinked the blood! Because of her fear Caroline turned on the TV. By watching it for about an hour she ceased to think about the blood and then fell asleep. But at the moment she was unaware that she and her husband were not alone in the cabin …

2.

July 16th

It was about 3.20 a.m. Moonlight was casting a haunting glare through the bedroom window, and it gave illumination to the room. There was total silence in the cabin. The only sound was low static emanating from the bedroom TV – Caroline had fallen asleep while she was watching it and the broadcast had ended hours ago. The couple was sleeping calmly. Up to this point of time the wife had been dreaming peacefully, but then suddenly something weird happened: Caroline was dreaming that she was lying on the sofa downstairs. It was night and she was nearly unable to see around her since the lights were out. She got herself up and started to grope in the dark – touching the door frames to find the switch. It was difficult since she didn't know the exact location. The reason was that during the previous day it hadn't been necessary for her to use the switch downstairs since the sun had given its light the whole day.

Caroline searched for the light switch a couple of minutes – which from her point of view felt like a couple of hours – but then her search came to a sudden end: a sound came from the bedroom upstairs! She heard it and it caused chills all over her body:

CLIP!

CLIP!

Caroline prayed she hadn't heard that sound. But she had heard it loud and clear – and she recognized it all too well: it was the cut sound of a pair of scissors! This thought caused her heartbeat to rise. She was unaware to who was cutting with the scissors, and – the worst part – what was being cut with them. A great horror came over Caroline for her husband who had been asleep in the bed. She tried to calm down herself by thinking that the sound didn't come from a pair of scissors by necessity. Instantly the dreadful sound came again from the dark:

CLIP!

CLIP!

No, she was not mistaken – it was the sound of a pair of cutting scissors! The wife was feeling the grip of an increasing amount of fear. She begun ascending the stairs hastily but quietly, since she didn't want to draw the attention of the person using the scissors. While going up Caroline felt her pulse increasing by each step she took. Finally she was standing in front of the bedroom door, which was open a little bit. She decided to take a peek in the room and see if her husband was in danger. If necessary, she could strike the cutter with the candle holder which she had grabbed from the downstairs cabinet – by her instict, without thinking about it.

Caroline encouraged herself, took a deep breath and peeked through the narrow opening of the door. At first she was looking for her beloved Steven from the right-side mattress on which he had been sleeping. She felt a relief when she noticed her husband was nowhere to be seen. She opened the door entirely and then stepped inside the bedroom – seeing the whole room and the double bed. What she saw next was something that made her paralyzed with fear: she saw the scissors which were used for cutting, and also that the left-side mattress of the bed was being cut with them – around its lower left corner – but she saw no-one who cut with the scissors – she wasn't sure there even was anyone! The scissors were cutting a big, circular hole near the lower left corner of the mattress – they had already cut the hole for a quarter of a circle. Suddenly they started to move and cut the mattress, and once again the night air was pierced with the horrific sound:

CLIP!

CLIP!

Caroline was startled so greatly that she gave a loud scream from her throat. In an instant she woke up and saw herself to be lying on the bed – soaked with sweat and panting. The dream she had seen was in her memory all too clear. Alarmingly the wife looked at the lower part of the mattress – while praying that there was nothing to be seen. To her relief she noticed no cuttingmarks of any kind on the mattress. Then she determined the vision had been just a bad dream.

Caroline saw her dear husband sleeping next to her in peace, and she decided to go back to sleep. While she was thinking this her sight met the TV opposite the bed – which was still producing low static. At first she saw just the usual static spots which appear after every

transmission. But after a little while Caroline started to
see someting unusual: she thought there appeared a
person on the TV! She then rubbed her eyes since she
thought they were playing tricks on her. When she
looked the TV screen again, there was no more room
for any mistake: from the middle of the static the lines
of a fuzzy human figure started to emerge!

When this sight faced Caroline she was so
frightened that she started screaming and covered her
face with her hands. Her husband woke up quickly and
rose to sitting on the bed. Steven was greatly startled
due to his wife's screaming in the middle of the night.
He was also perplexed seeing Caroline sitting on the
bed crying and pointing with her finger at the static TV
screen. Steven was unable to figure out what was
wrong with the TV. But then his wife him there had
been a person on the screen in the middle of the static.
After hearing this the husband started assuring her that
all of this had been just a nightmare which was now
over and gone. Steven embraced Caroline, kissed her,
ran his fingers through her long tresses and caressed her
breasts. After some time she was feeling much relieved.
Steven got up and turned off the static TV. Then he
went back to the bed, lied down and soon fell asleep
again.

Despite her husband's words Caroline was unable
to think everything had been just a nightmare – she
knew what she had seen with her own eyes! The wife
was still unable to find peace from her thoughts. She
decided to get up and look inside the upper drawer of
the night stand to check if the scissors were still there –
Steven had cleaned the blood and then placed the
scissors inside this drawer. With shaking hands
Caroline opened the drawer and looked inside: the

scissors were there. After noticing this her mind was calmed to the extent that she was feeling sleepy. She went back to the bed, lied down next to her husband and fell asleep. However, the visions of the cutting scissors and the fuzzy human figure were very present in her conciousness ...

3.

July 16th

In the morning – about 9.30 a.m. – Steven got up. Through the bedroom window he noticed the sun was shining and the birds were singing – and this raised up his spirit. He saw Caroline was still sleeping. At first he thought waking her, but then decided to let her sleep; it came back to him that his wife had seen a terrible nightmare last night, so she would need more sleep than him. After he got dressed up Steven went to the kitchen for some breakfast. Half an hour passed and the time came to 10.00 a.m. on the clock. From downstairs came sounds of clinging and banging – with the smell of food – to the bedroom. Then also Caroline began to wake up. Half-asleep she got sitting on the bed – only to change her position right away since the sun was shining straight upon her eyes. But this woke her up fully. First she walked to the window and looked through it. After Caroline saw how beautiful was the day outside, she felt her mood brightened in an instant. Yes, she did remember the horrific vision from last night, but now she thought it had been just her mind playing tricks on her. Yes, this had to be so! The scissors cutting the mattress on their own were just a nightmare, and the figure on the TV was just a hallucination caused by this bad dream.

In high spirits Caroline got dressed and went downstairs. When she got to the kitchen she greeted her beloved Steven, who in turn gave her a plate filled with breakfast – fried eggs and bacon – and a cup of hot coffee. She then sat at the table and begun her first meal of the day. Her husband had already finished his own, so he decided to go out for some fresh air. When Steven left the kitchen, he pulled the room door almost closed, but left it open just a bit. The wife was eating with good appetite and thinking about what they could do today. After a while she was almost finished with her morning meal. While she was in her thoughts Caroline was looking at the small mirror on the western wall of the kitchen – just opposite the door. By looking at this mirror she saw the door suddenly opening. Then she turned her head toward the door – thinking it was just her husband coming back. At first the door was opening slowly – but then it flung wide open! Caroline was terrified: there was no-one at the door! It was then her mind was again flooded with all the horrors of last night. She tried to calm herself and block these frightening ideas by saying to herself it had been just the wind. But in reality she didn't even believe in this explanation: only a very powerful gust would be able to flung the door open like that, but the wind was seemigly wery mild outside. So she tried to turn her attention elsewhere: Caroline looked towards the southern wall of the room – just opposite her. This wall was covered all over with white wallpaper and there was a tiny picture hanging on it – the sun shining through the window on the northern wall gave its light upon it. It was toward this wall she directed her sight and was expecting to see just her own shadow on it. This was natural since she saw no-one else in the room.

Indeed, the wife saw her own shadow – but to her horror also a second one, the shadow of a totaly unknown person! She was startled and looked behind her: there was no-one to be seen! In fright she turned her sight back to the wall, and the other shadow was there. It was then Caroline thought there had to be someone else in the room – someone who could not be seen! By shaking and sweating the wife looked at the shadow. Suddenly the figure started to move: it walked slowly and slumping from the door towards the little mirror on the opposite wall of the room. After she determined that the unseen figure stood in front of the mirror, she turned and looked at the mirror. She then saw something odd: the surface of the mirror began to be covered by moist! Caroline was watching this event with curiosity but also with fear – apparently it was the shadowy figure's breath which was causing this! Finally the mirror was fully covered with moist. Then came about something which was only terrifying: Caroline turned back towards the wall in order to see if the figure was still standing at the mirror. It was and was also touching the mirror with it's finger. In an instant she heard a scratching sound from behind her! After hearing this she was overcome with dread and horror. She was scared to look at the mirror again – if there had appeared something on it, the shadowy figure would be real! Despite her fear Caroline was still looking at the shadow on the wall – while trying not to hear the scratching sound which came about every time the figure moved its finger on the mirror.

Finally the unknown thing took its finger off the mirror and was standing in front of it – as if looking at its own reflection. Caroline felt her fear increasing and her heart pounding on full strength. She was paraying and sobbingly wishing that Steven would already come back inside – but he wasn't showing up. However, in the midst of her despair she was still able to think; if the scratching noise she had just heard was indeed caused by the figure, it would be really existing. Even though this increased her pain even more, she grabbed the coffee cup on the table. She had decided to encourage herself and tried to strike the figure's head with this cup; it would probably be so distracted that she could escape the kitchen and reach her Steven. By this plan she was able encourage herself – however still in fear – and was grabbing the cup even tightly. Caroline then looked at the shadow, and saw the thing still standing at the mirror. She was just about to toss the cup when the figure suddenly turned its head. She was in terror – the shadowy figure was now looking right at her! Her fear kept on growing, but she was thinking fast: the wife took a deep breath, looked at the shadow, turned quickly and then tossed the cup by her right hand towards the desired spot. She was expecting the cup to hit something invisible to the eye. To her horror this didn't come to pass: the cup hit the wall on the opposite side and it shattered to pieces. Caroline was greatly startled by this, since she had been confident the cup would hit the head of the figure standing at the mirror. It was then she looked at the mirror itself – the one she had heard was being scratched a while ago. There was indeed a real mark on the mirror! This was a clear proof that someone else was in the room. At first she was unable to believe her own eyes. Then she looked more closely and was met by a creepy sight: on the mirror there was a real mark drawn by human blood!

After seeing this there came cries of horror out of her mouth – like molten lava out of a volcano. She instantly got up and tried to get out of the kitchen as soon as possible. In this terror she was unable to pay attention to her surrondings: after getting out of the kitchen door she tripped to the carpet edge, fell over and struck her temple against the cabinet edge. She felt her conciousness blurring and fainted in the middle of the hall. She fell into the dark.

It is unknown how long Caroline was in blackout. The first thing she remembered after the fall was her lying on the sofa and having a prickling pain on her head. To relieve the pain Steven had taken a bag of vegetables out of the freezer and placed it on her forehead. It was also her dear husband who had carried her on the sofa to recover. He was upstairs watching TV, but as soon as he heard the wife calling he rushed downstairs. At first he was just glad to see Caroline was awake. However, he soon began to wonder what had happened to her while he was outside. The wife – being still a bit dizzy due to her fall – was also wondering it herself. She tried to remember what had happened before the fall, but it was of no use: there was a black veil over her memory, and it was not possible to see through it. To Steven this didn't come as a surprise – after all, it is very common that a person who has fainted due to head injury doesn't remember anything of the time preceding the event. Caroline got up and went to the kitchen for some refreshing drink. After re-entering the kitchen she opened the fridge – on the right side of the mirror – grabbed a bottle of orange juice, took a glass off the shelf and filled it with the juice. Then she sat at the table – again facing the southern wall – and started to sip her cold juice.

As the wife was drinking she started to fall into ther thoughts. Soon her sight started to wander and go around across the kitchen wall – just like everyone who has nothing better to do. Caroline didn't see anything noteworthy on the wall illumined by the sunshine: just her own shadow and the little picture on the wall. Vaimo ei aluksi nähnytkään auringon valaisemalla seinällä mitään muuta katsomisen arvoista kuin oman varjonsa ja seinällä olevan pienen taulun. But then – all of a sudden – her eyes behold something else – something that tore apart the black veil over her memory and released all the memories buried behind it that now became a chilling reality: she saw another shadow on the wall besides her own! In a flash she recalled it to be the same figure she tried to strike a moment ago. But this situation was a lot more frightening: the thing was sitting at the table, right next to her! After the wife saw this she was paralyzed and shaking with fear. She wasn't even able to call her husband who had gone back upstairs.

While Caroline was panicking over what to do, there came a weird feeling over her: she started to chill and get cold – it was freezing! This got her so startled that she turned her head to see what was happening at her right sides. Quickly and frightfully she turned her head and looked: there was no-one to be seen at her side – just as she had expected. But the spot on the bench itself was changed: it was covered with human blood! Just the sight of this got her shivering all the more. Suddenly she got the feeling that cold was spreading on her face. She then looked back at the wall and was met by a horrible sight: The shadow thing had turned its head and was now staring right at her! Caroline was now feeling the thing's breathing upon her face! This terrible sight and realization made the wife to scream in horror. Soon was heard the sound of the stairs, and her husband rushed into the kitchen. After Steven met Caroline weeping, she started telling him what had happened – about the shadowy figure leaving a bloody mark on the mirror – with a miserable voice and with eyes full of tears. Steven went to the mirror and looked at it very closely: there was no blood on the mirror – it was perfectly clean!

Caroline kept on with her story. Then she told him about the thing sitting next to her and bleeding on the bench. Steven looked at the bench: it was also all clean, without any traces of blood! He was very confused over all this; he wasn't able to comprehed what had gotten to his wife – she had never said anything like this before! It was alltogether impossible for Steven to believe there had been an invisible shadow figure in the kitchen. But he loved his wife deeply and wanted to trust her. Therefore he tried to make sense of all this: there might have been an intruder in the cabin, which his wife saw and thought to be invisible due to her concussion. Caroline wasn't satisfied by this explanation, but she decided to say nothing more – Steven couldn't believe anything more. However, he did believe to such an extent that he opened the suitcase and took out a handgun – he had brought it alongside for their safety. He placed it on the downstairs cabinet and hid it under a hat. In this way he wanted to make sure that if the unwanted guest – whoever it might be – came back, he and his wife would be able to defend themselves. Steven thought he had now taken care of any danger. Caroline, however, felt it was still present in the air ...

4.

July 16th

Caroline felt herself somewhat relaxed and she was able to finish her breakfast. After this she and her husband went for a walk in the nearby forest. When the couple returned to the cabin, they went to the bedroom upstairs. Caroline and Steven took off their clothes, kissed each other and made love with passion – which was followed by a rest for a couple hour of hours.

It was about 5.15 p.m. when the couple woke up. The first thought they had was this: to go for their first swim in the crystal lake! Steven and Caroline got up and dressed up in a while; he was wearing dark-blue swim trunks and she put on her red bikini. After grabbing some towels they went outside and walked to the lakeshore – by a path with stone pavement – with high spirits. They reached the docks. Steven was filled with boy-like excitement and jumped into the water. Caroline followed him, but feelling modesty she used the stairs to get to the lake. The water was clean and warm – just the way she liked it. After a while Steven got out of the water and lay himself down on the boards for sunbathing. But his wife wanted to keep on swimming – for she found it very refreshing and relieving. The day was also at its finest: the sun was shining, the birds were singing and the sky was bright blue.

While swimming Caroline didn't notice she had gotten some distance between her and Steven – about a hundred feet. She then took notice and decided to swim back to him. But she was distracted by a weird feeling: the water around her – up to this moment nice and warm – suddenly began to feel much colder! This puzzled her and she thought it must be a cold current from the bottom of the lake. Very soon the water had become so freezing she was shivering and decided to swim back to the shore. But as soon as she begun her swim, she had a dreadful feeling upon her right foot: something had taken hold of it! Caroline was scared to death, for she felt it was a human hand grabbing her foot! This, however, didn't feel like the hand of a living human being: it was cold, sticky and bony – like the hand of a corpse! In fear Caroline yelled and shook her leg violently. The underwater grip was thight, but then she struck the hand with her left heel and it let go. In an instant the water was warm again. Steven – awakened by his wife – had jumped back to the lake and was swimming towards her. She was swimming towards the shore as quickly as possible – like in a peril. He met her at about 50 feet off the shore, but she went right pass him: with tears pouring out of her eyes she was swimming to the docks – with no intent of slowing her pace. Steven was wondering this as he followed Caroline. After they reached the docks and got out of the lake he was asking her what had happened.

At first she remained silent – being very exhausted and frightened. But after a while she was able to tell her husband the hand grabbing her foot underwater. Steven said it had most likely been just some plant or wooden branch lying on the lake bottom. But she insisted it had been a human hand. To this he replied it was just nonsense, keeping his own opinion. Hearing this caused her to burst into tears, but he then embraced his wife – and soon her sobbing ceased. Caroline and her husband came back to the shore. However, Steven was inclined to prove her fear to be unnecessary. There was a little boat next to the docks; so he untied it, got seated and began to row. When the boat had reached the desired spot, he took a fishing net and started to reach the bottom of the lake with it. At first he found nothing, but finally the net caught something. Caroline – standing on the shore and observing the efforts of her husband – was greatly startled when Steven said there was something in the net. As he was bringing the net back to the surface, she felt her pulse gettting higher. But her fear was relieved after she could see what it was: just a branch of pine! To Steven this was what he needed to prove his wife to be mistaken: it had been this branch that caught her foot and she had falsely thought it was a hand. Steven turned the boat and started rowing back to the shore. Caroline, however, was still obseving that particular spot of the lake. She didn't want to argue with her husband anymore – but she did still think it had been a human hand!

After Steven got back to the shore he and his wife returned to the cabin to cook dinner – spaghetti and meatballs. They ate their fill and had a rest. When they had woken up the couple went again for a walk in the forest. They also had a nice trip at the lake by the boat. Once the time was about 9.30 p.m., Caroline and Steven decided to go sleeping. But as soon as they had gotten to the bed, she got scared: it was due to the turned-on TV. She told her husband about the fuzzy figure she had seen on the TV last night and was afraid to go sleeping – she had already told her husband about this vision, but she wasn't sure he would remember it anymore. Steven was wondering why Caroline was so worried about her nightmare. He tried to comfort his wife, but she refused. So he went to the TV, turned it off and pulled the socket off the wall. After climbing back to the bed he reassured her that it had been just her imagination. Steven laid his head upon the pillow – and he was soon asleep. But his wife wasn't able to sleep: there was a horrifying thought forming itself in her mind – that the events of this day, the last night visions and the bed mattress were related in some weird way! This creepy idea was circling itself around her head for a some time. Finally she decided it would be better to think about these things on the next day – at night imagination can mess up one's thoughts. In order to get some sleep she tried to think other, more positive things. After about half an hour she fell asleep – but not in peace. Caroline was unaware that soon after she fell asleep some eerie things started to occur in the room: the bedroom door – nearly closed – was opened and the sound of steps was heard in the room – with no visible form to be seen ...

5.
July 17th

It was 2.30 a.m. Even though it was dark outside the full moon was bringing forth its light through the bedroom window. This illumined the room quite a bit. Steven and Caroline were sleeping – totally unaware of what was going on in the room. The husband was sleeping very peacefully, but his wife was restless. She was having a strange dream: she was standing in the middle of the pathway she and Steven had walked yesterday. She was wearing her nightgown and her feet were bare. It was night, but due to the moonlight she could see around her quite well. Caroline was looking at the nocturnal forest. At first she saw no-one, so she thought to be alone. But suddenly she saw someone – or something – moving behind one of the pines next to the path. She got very startled, because she was unaware who or what it was. She was looking intently at the tree behind which she had seen movement.

Then Caroline saw something that paralyzed her with fear: an unknown woman stepped slowly out from behind the tree! Her form was attractive, the hair on her head was long and blonde, and she was wearing a blue dress. But all this was mixed with some very horrifying features: the woman's face and her dress were stained with human blood, and there was a blood-dripping hole where her left eye was supposed to be! After seeing this Caroline was so terrified she cried as much as she could. But no sound was coming out of her mouth. Terror and anxiety were growing and growing – she didn't know what to do. She didn't dare to look at the creepy woman – presumably still standing next to the tree – and so the wife turned her back to her. She then started to walk – slowly and straight forward – along the path which was covered by pine needles. Caroline was walking towards the direction she knew the cabin was. She was looking intently towards the ground, because she didn't dare to look around her – and especially behind her! Now she was determined to get to the cabin as soon as possible and tell her husband. With this thought the wife was walking rapidly on the path – with great distress and her heart pounding inside her chest.

For some time Caroline walked and then halted; she was thinking it would now be safe to look around a bit – the cabin was supposed to be nearby. She slowly lifted her eyes from the ground and looked forward her: to her horror she saw nothing but dark forest – with the endless looking path slithering forward like a snake and disappearing to its bottomless, deep, black maw! Then it came to her mind: the terrifying thought of going the path the wrong way and being now even deeper in the forest than before! This process of thinking was making Caroline feel increasing fright and terror. And then she remembered the unknown woman she had seen just a while ago: Caroline was unaware if she had followed her – she might be standing right behind her back! Her fear was increasing and her forehead was dripping with cold sweat. She began to think what to do next. At first she thought it would be out of the question to look behind her; if the woman stood behind her, it would be impossible to know what might happen. But finally she decided to turn around. Caroline took a deep breath, swallowed, turned and looked behind her – prepared to see the bloody woman staring at her with the single eye!

But no-one was to be seen anywhere – just dark woods. She felt a bit lighter after seeing her expectation had been false: apparently the creepy woman had stayed far behind and had not followed her after all. She would now be able to go back to the cabin – and her beloved Steven. Since her fear had now eased a bit, she decided to keep going and turned around.

Caroline was then met with a shock of terror: the woman was standing right before her – dressed in the blue-colored, bloody dress and staring at her with one eye! The wife got so scared that she fell to the ground – screaming and shaking hysterically. The creepy woman was standing before her with no expressions and totally still – just staring at her. She was twisting in terror on the ground, until it finally came to an end. Caroline was lying on her back and looking at the bloody face of the woman – expecting her to do something horrible.

They stared at each other for a while. But then – all of a sudden – the woman started to move! With some short steps she walked right next to the fear-paralyzed Caroline, who was shaking as with a seizure and staring at the blue-dressed woman even more intently. But then happened something very unexpected: the woman bent down and reached Caroline with her hand! At first she was wondering this gesture with feelings wixed with fear: she didn't dare to touch the hand. It was then she turned her eyes to see her face and was amazed to see it had changed: the face – just a moment ago so cold and unfeeling – had now become gentle and friendly, even smiling at her! It was this sight that gave her courage to hold on to the woman's hand – despite still having great fear. Caroline got support and was able to get back on her feet. What had happened was puzzling her and she found it to be both fascinating and frightening at the same time; the bloody woman was still standing before her, but she didn't seem as horrifying as before.

Suddenly the woman started to walk away from her, leaving the path and stepping right towards the dark forest. Caroline was calling after the woman, but she got no answer. She wanted to find out who the woman was, so she decided to follow. She went behind her through the woods for some time. Finally the woman stopped all of a sudden at one particular tree: it was a very old pine with deformed figure and twisted branches. The woman walked to the tree and stood before it. Caroline stayed at some distance off to see what the woman would do – she really began to wonder what was going on. Then the unknown woman suddenly turned around and started to stare at Caroline again. This went on for some time. But then the woman lifted her left hand and was pointing at the wife with a finger – causing Caroline to startle a bit. After a while the woman moved her left hand so it was now pointing at the base of the tree – one very specific spot in it. Caroline was very puzzed and she asked the woman what was the meaning of this. But then – at the very moment – her dream was changing: instead of the dark forest Caroline was now standing in the hall of the dark cabin, right before the cabinet. She was getting an intuition of what would happen next – and this made her heart to beat more and more rapidly …

6.
July 17th

Caroline was standing in the middle of the cabin hall. Before her there was the cabinet and behind her was the sofa. She was standing still and looking around her very nervously. Even though is was night, moonlight gave illumination so she was able to see around her. There was no-one to be seen in the hall and the deadly silence was everywhere. The wife's fear was increasing: she did remember her dream last night. It had begun excatly the same way and had come to an end by the terrible vision of the scissors cutting the mattress on their own. Her thoughts were at this very spot, and then she heard in the darkness the sound – the one having echoed in her ears as a haunting memory just a moment ago, but now it was present as part of the cold reality:

CLIP!

CLIP!

Hearing this sound almost stopped her heart of fear and terror; the last night vision of the scissors cutting on their own was even stronger in her mind! Caroline was overcome by this terror for some time. But finally she was able to take heart and decided to enter the bedroom upstairs – judging by her vision from last night she would be able to expect what was going to happen in the room. The wife stepped before the cabinet and took the handgun her husband had hidden there. Then she removed the safety and began ascending the stairs in a slow and cautious manner.

While Caroline was ascending the stairs she was thinking what she would do after entering the room. First of all she would make sure Steven was fine, but if he was sleeping in the bed his life could be in danger. Then she would aim the gun at the cutter's arm or leg – maybe invisible but still real – and shoot it. This would cause the cutter to drop the scissors and would not be able to do anything due to the pain. This would give her the chance to save her husband and escape the unseen threat. Thinking like this gave her some courage. She had reached the bedroom door – slightly opened – and was standing right at it. She placed her hand against the door and was about to open it – then suddenly the sound came out of the room once more:

CLIP!

CLIP!

The wife could feel the terror raising its head once again and was unable to open the door. A creepy idea had just entered her mind: what if the cutter and the shadowy figure in the kitchen were the one and the same entity! She was hesitating to use the gun since it wasn't clear to her who – or what – it was. Despite all this she decided to shoot, however, because she was unable to think anything else. Caroline encouraged herself and opened the bedroom door. She opened it very slowly to see if her beloved husband was fine. She opened the door just enough to see the right side of the bed: Steven wasn't in the bed and therefore not threatened. This observation calmed her down a bit – to such an extent she was able to open he door fully and step inside the room.

Even this courage was unable to prepare her for the horrifying vision now opening before her eyes. To some extent it was the same vision as last night: she did see the scissors cutting the mattress on their own – at the same exact spot as before. The rest of it, however, was something she was totally unprepared to see. She had been expecting the cutter to be invisible, but this assumption was wrong: now she was able to see the one cutting! Shock came over Caroline: she saw someone sitting on the left mattress – laying on knees and cutting a circular hole at the mattress' lower left corner. She was unable to see the cutter's appearance due to the dark, but the outer lines of the figure could be seen: it was clear enough to determine the figure was formed as a human! Caroline was shaking violently and looking at the figure in the darkness. Apparently it hadn't noticed her and so kept on cutting the mattress slowly. She could feel her terror and unawareness growing by each second. And then the chilling sound was heard again in the room:

CLIP!

CLIP!

Once again the shadowy figure cut through the mattress. It had already cut the hole about a three-quarter size of a full circle. It was then Caroline did it: by an instinct she lifted the handgun up and fired three shots at the figure's right hand which was holding the scissors. The bullets pierced its right arm but it didn't even writhe! Seeing this paralyzed the wife with fear and so she dropped the gun on the floor.

But then – all of a sudden – the figure stopped cutting the mattress and turned its face straight towards Caroline. She was then able to notice a detail she had previously been unable to see: she saw in the figure's face just the right eye – the left one was totally gone! The cutter was now looking at the wife with its only eye – it was blood-red and burning with wrath. The wife was terrifed by that dark figure looking at her – totally still and surrounded by deep silence. All of a sudden something horrible happened: the shadow figure lifted its right arm and threw the scissors right at Caroline! She closed her eyes for fear – followed by a whirling sound and a burning pain in her chest. This ended the dream and she woke up – scared and stressed. She was still tired due to the events of yesterday, so after seeing it had been a bad dream she went back to sleep almost right away. However, if she had been awake a little longer, she might have noticed something in the room that was changed during the night ...

7.

July 17th

The night went peacefully from this moment forward –
for both Caroline and Steven. It was about 10.30 a.m.
when he woke up. He got up, took his clothes from the
nearby chair and dressed up. The husband then decided
to look though the window to see what kind of a day it
would be – after this he would go to the kitchen to
make some breakfast. But little did Steven know this
intention of his would be done only by the first half: at
first he checked the window and saw the weather to be
nice and without any clouds. He got cheered up by this
– since at the following night there would be the lunar
eclipse and the weather seemed to be perfect for
observing it. But his enthusiasm was shortlived: just as
he was walking to the bedroom door, he turned his eyes
towards Caroline who was still sleeping in peace. But
then Steven saw the wall above the bed – just opposite
the window – and he got truly disturbed: someone had
entered the bedroom while they were sleeping and had
drawn a bloody mark on the wall!

He could feel great fear and insecurity taking over his
whole mind: who had done this? Almost instantly he
got the thought that his wife had drawn on the wall.

Steven stepped next to his sleeping wife and woke her up. She was startled and drowsy – and was wondering what was going on. When his husband told her to take a look at the wall above her, she lifted her sight and was terrified; it was the very same mark she had seen drawn on the kitchen mirror yesterday! Caroline decided right away it had been the same shadow figure who had been at the kitchen. When she thought of this, she began weeping and embraced her husband. Steven was a bit scared due to his wife's reaction. After she had calmed down he asked if she had drawn the mark on the wall. But when she heard this she burst again into tears and insisted it hadn't been her. She then told him the mark had been drawn by the thing she had seen at the kitchen in the yesterday morning.

Caroline's answer convinced Steven that she was innocent; it strongly seemed there had been a third guest at the house – the uninvited one. He thought they should be even more careful from now on – after all, it was not possible to know the intruder's intensions. But the wife thought those intensions were somehow connected with the blood. She, however, decided to keep this idea to herself – to keep Steven from worrying too much. Her husband went to the nightstand – on which the TV was – and took a key out of the drawer. He put the key to the keyhole of the bedroom door; Steven had decided that from now on they would lock the door for safety. Then also his wife got up and dressed herself up. They went downstairs together for breakfast and decided to forget that frightening moment. The day was just starting and they wanted it to be more pleasant than yesterday.

From the moment of breakfast on the day was going much more peaceful than the day before. After they had breakfast Caroline and Steven went for a swim. Then they went fishing by boat, prepared lunch and ate their fill. After finishing the meal they went upstairs together and enjoyed making love in the bed. In the afternoon – about 1.30 p.m. – the wife decided to go for a little walk in the forest – for the weather outside was beautiful once again. She put on her outdoor clothes and went on her way. At first she walked on the pathway going through the woods and her walk was going smoothly. After about 15 minutes she was already quite deep in the forest. She had just finished the circulating part of the path and was now at the spot leasing to the long, straight part. The wife was walking in calm pace and at the same time was looking around her – observing the summer forest. All around her there was green, the birds were singing and the sun was shining. It was indeed a fine day and she was in high spirits. She let her eyesight wander among the endless rows of trees.

It was then Caroline saw a peculiar tree which brought her much confusion: there was an old pine tree with very twisted branches. She remembered her dream last night: she had followed the strange, bloody woman to a pine just like this one! At first there was s lot of doubt on her mind: it just looked like the dream tree but most definetely it couldn't be the same one! In order to be sure she started to walk towards the tree so she could take a look at it.

Caroline went to the tree. She started to go around it, observing the trunk and branches as she went. Now she was the tree as the one in her dream – even the branches had the exact same shape. Therefore she began to think there was something special about that tree. So the wife decided to inspect the tree very carefully – it might even give some answers to the creepy events and visions of the previous days. In the tree itself there was nothing unusual. But suddenly Caroline remembered what the woman in the blue dress had done in the dream: she had pointed the ground around the tree. The wife began to observe the ground and soon she noticed something: there was a black leather strap protruding out of the ground. She bowed down and saw it was the carrying strap of a bag. She took hold of it and pulled – only to notice it was fast and tight in the ground. Therefore she began to dig the soil around the leather strap. Finally she found the object to which it was fastened: there was a black, leather handbag buried under the tree. This bag was partly decayed and seemed to be somewhat old. After finding the bag Caroline thought right away this was what the woman in the dream had meant. She decided to take it with her to the cabin; there she would be able to check its contents with her husband and think what all of this was. She lifted the bag up and started to walk back to the cabin in rapid pacing.

It was about 2.45 p.m. when Caroline got back to the cabin with the handbag. After entering it she began to call Steven. But then she checked the time and it came to her that he had told about visiting the nearby village at that time. Therefore she decided to check the bag by herself. She went to the kitchen and sat at the table. She then placed the bag on the table and opened it: there was a lot of mildew inside, but she didn't let this distract her. She turned the bag over and poured its contents to the table: a number of small items spread on the table. In the midst of these was dirt and tiny insects – these got scared of the light and ran in panic all over the table. Caroline began to separate items from the trash – and she found many kinds of items: a comb, some lipstick, a powder box, lotion and a pack of tissues. Among the items was also a string of colorful beads with the image of the crucified attached to it – Caroline understood these were rosary beads. Finally she found a small, oval locket made of porcelain – its sides were shining. She decided to open this locket: its cover slid open, revealing a photo inside. It was a wedding photo: a husband with his bride. After seeing this Caroline began to look more closely what they looked like: the man was wearing a black suit, he was quite tall and handsome. His hair was dark and straight, he had a mustache and was wearing a pair of glasses. The woman was wearing a white wedding dress, she was very delicate and clearly shorter than her husband. Her hair was long and blonde, and her face was pretty. It didn't take Caroline long to realize something terrifying: the bride of the photo looked just like the woman from her dream! The resemblance was so obvious – even without the left eyeball – she was unable to avoid the impression that the bride of the photo was indeed the woman she had seen in her dream! She got anxious and the question on her mind was: who is that woman?

Caroline began to ponder the question right away. She figured the couple in the photo would probably have been previously at the cabin she and Steven were now. And if this were the case, their real estate agent might know something about it. So she went to the bedroom upstairs, took the agent's card out of her handbag and came back downstairs with it. Then she picked up the receiver of the phone – on the table next to the sofa, at the right side of the bathroom. After dialing the number she called and waited for the answer. In a while the agent picked up the phone. Caroline put forward her issue and questioned how many people had rented the cabin before her and her husband. The agent had records for the last 15 years. He checked them and after some time came back to the phone. He found out there had only been one instance when this place was rented during this time: it had been a married couple over 10 years ago. When Caroline heard this, she asked the agent about them and their appearance – while holding the wedding photo in her hand. Once again he checked the register and began to give her the info on the phone. Caroline heard their names – Robert and Suzan – and after the agent had given the description of them she noticed it was matching with the photo. Finally she wanted to know where the couple was at the moment. The agent told her the husband was living in his hometown. But the bride's fate sounded to be terrible to her: according to Robert his wife Suzan was captured at this cabin, and he was afraid she had been killed! This caused her to get really anxious. However, she didn't mention anything about the visions she had seen. So Caroline gave thanks to the agent and closed the call.

When the call was over, she sat still on the sofa for some time; she was totally unable to say what was happening around her. She took another look at the photo. Caroline wasn't able to stop thinking about the things the agent had said concerning the woman of the picture. The fact she was presumably dead scared her the most. Could the blue-dressed woman really be Suzan? While she was thinking about this she began pondering how this could be. At first she rationalized the matter: the bride would be still alive, after she had escaped the kidnapper and finally ended up back here.

However – due to her visions – Caroline was unable to avoid the thought the woman in the photo was really dead. This gave her a chill: in that case the woman she had encountered was a living dead – an undead person! She got so terrified that all of a sudden the memory from yesterday came back to her: it was the shadow thing at the kitchen! At that moment Caroline remembered something terrifying: even though it had been impossible to see the details of the thing's looks, she could determine what its shadow looked like: it was quite clearly human – and very likely a woman! Caroline was thinking further: if the shadow figure and the woman in her dream were the same entity, she had indeed seen an undead person in the forest! Then she also remembered the thing in the kitchen had – judging by the shadow – long hair and was wearing a nightgown. This obsevation got her heart shivering with fear – and she couldn't take it any longer: she rushed to the door, put her shoes on, and went outside as soon as possible. Caroline ran to the docks and sat down on the bench there. She tried hard to calm herself down, but the fear was too strong. Therefore she made a decision: when her husband got back, they would pack their bags and leave this place right away. This thought relieved her a bit.

The wife sat on the bench, shivering with fear and waiting Steven to return. He drove with the car back to the cabin at about 3.30 p.m. – she had waited about half an hour. He got out and took the stuff he had bought from the back seat. Steven then saw his beloved Caroline running towards him. She met her husband crying and embraced him. He was confused and asked her what was the matter. She, however, didn't want to say anything about the dream last night, the photo ot the bride. Instead she talked to her husband directly: she was afraid of this place and wanted to leave – and this would be done today. At first Steven was reluctant, but finally he agreed – he had also been feeling uneasy about the cabin due to his wife's incidents. Caroline got relieved after hearing her beloved Steven agreed with her – and he also tried to calm her down. They walked to the porch and went inside to have some dinner. But neither of them noticed they were not alone even then: soon after they had entered the kitchen there were stepping sounds on the porch. Then the front door – just a bit open – was opening slowly without anyone noticing. Then the door was fully opened – and there was no-one to be seen. Only the sound of the steps was heard and a dark shadow cast itself on the hall floor …

8.
July 17th

Caroline and Steven began to pack their luggage when they had finished the dinner. After packing all their things – excluding the bedclothes – they felt tired and decided to have a rest before leaving. Caroline and her husband slept for a few hours – until 7.20 p.m. – in order to have the strength to watch the lunar eclipse on the following night. When the couple woke up they decided to take a shower together. In the bathroom they took off their clothes and went under the shower. Caroline gave Steven a kiss, knelt down and suck his cock. He was surprised – she had never done this before – but he didn't resist it. Steven came in her mouth and she swallowed it. He then decided to give her a surprise as well: after she rose up, he knelt down and reached Caroline's naked crotch with his face: Steven rubbed her bush with his nose, and then he began to use his tongue – licking his wife's pussy and sticking the tongue in her vagina. Caroline got even more surprised by her husband – and more pleasure: she was whining and squirming with pleasure. And then she also came – with a big squirt out of her pussy, all over her husband's face. After this Steven rose up, kissing her and rubbing his face all over hers. Caroline returned the favor by licking his face – and her own juice – and rubbing his cock with her right hand. To this Steven responded by caressing her crotch with his left hand. The couple was totally overwhelmed by sensuality and promiscuity; both of them weren't thinking about anything else but one's own pleasure –

and how to get more of it. This went on for about half an hour. Then they began to shower.

After a while Steven left the bathroom, wearing his robe. Caroline put on her own robe and went to the toilet – opposite the bathroom door. She stepped before the mirror, brushed her hair and dried them up. She also put some lotion on her face and hands. After this she took her toothbrush, squeezed some paste on it and brushed her teeth. While she was rinsing her mouth and put her face over the sink to spit out the water, her sight wandered off the reflection. Then – all of a sudden – the toilet door behind her opened and she heard the threshold creak. She turned towards the door – assuming it was her husband – but there was no-one. At first she was wondering this, but then decided it had been her imagination – giving some peace for her thoughts.

Caroline turned back and looked right at the mirror – expecting to see just her own reflection. How wrong she was! What she saw in the mirror wasn't her own self but an unknown one – a woman with a horrible appearance: her skin was grey, lifeless and moldy. Her blue dress was soaking wet – just like her blonde hair. Her dress was winkled and stained with mud. Her arms and legs were covered with blood all over. Her face was full of open, bleeding wounds. The woman had just one eyeball – the right one, dripping blood – and with it she was staring intently at Caroline. At the same time blood was pouring out of her left, empty eyesocket – dripping over her face and blue dress. The woman's head was leaning backwards. Her mouth was opening and grinning with a creepy smile – all the while her only eyeball was bulking out of her head and staring.

Caroline was looking at the hideous thing in the mirror – with the heinous grin on its face and staring at her with its bloody eyeball. She was gripped with such a terror it gave her a shock: she was shaking all over and crying out – chanting it wasn't her in the mirror. At that moment she realized what she and Steven had done to each other in the bathroom – and felt guilty for it. She felt like her head was bursting and she collapsed on the floor. The wife was laying with no conciousness and totally unaware of what was happening around her. After she had passed out, the lights in the room went out. After this the sound of stepping was heard – followed by scratching from the direction of the mirror. When the scratching had ended, the threshold creaked and the door was closed – by no-one to be seen. The room was left with the silence of death. Caroline was laying unconciouss on the floor – *alone in the dark*.

She was blacked out for about half an hour. It was then she finally heard her beloved husband's voice calling her. She opened her eyes and saw Steven on his knees at her side – on the toilet floor. At first Caroline felt dizzy, but was recovering quite soon. When her husband was helping her to get up, she suddenly felt pain on her right arm. She looked at the arm and was starteled: it was bound with a blood-stained bandage! She also noticed there was something unpleasant on the floor: a pair of nail-trimmers in a small puddle of blood! Steven tried to calm her and told what happened: when he had found her laying on the floor there had been a deep bleeding wound on her right arm – and he had used some bandage to bind it. Caroline gave thanks to her husband, but he wasn't touched by this; he was questioning her who had cut the wound – and she tried to convince him she had no clue who it was. While she was talking with Steven, her eyes went unconciously back to the mirror to look at it. She was disturbed when she saw it: the same bloody mark had been drawn on the mirror!

In an instant – like a flash of lightning – there was an image before her internal eyes: that horrible, grinning woman in the mirror! Caroline began to panic and cry – leaping out of the toilet. She threw herself on the sofa and started weeping. Steven followed her and sat next to his wife. She was trying to wipe the bloody, grinning face off her mind, but it was hopeless: that face was persistently staying in her thoughts – perhaps forevermore!

Steven laid his hand on her wife's shoulder and she got up to sit on the sofa. Caroline began to tell him – in a sobbing and miserable tone – what had happened: she told about the thing in the mirror and insisted it had been the one who cut the wound and drew the bloody mark. Caroline also insisted it had been the same woman who appeared in the kitchen yesterday, drew the mark on the bedroom wall and had appeared in her dream – and it was then Steven had heard enough and he lost his nerve. In his mind there were fighting two opposite scenarios: in the first one his wife would be a liar and the one who made the bloody marks and the wound – not an "invisible" woman. In the other she would be telling the truth and the culprit was some unknown, hostile being. The conflict between the two scenarios was very obvious – they could not be fitted together. Steven felt his own concept of the reality to become blurry – apparently this had already happened to his wife. He told her that apparently they both were under the same mental illness and they would go and see a psychiatrist right after they got home. She got frightened by this talk and insisted she was totally healthy – blaming the bloody woman for everything. But Steven was unwilling to hear about it anymore. Instead he suggested they would go to sleep now and leave in the morning; it was already dark outside and they were both too nervous to travel.

Caroline and Steven went to the bedroom and locked the door. She put the TV on and he set the alarm to go off at 4.13 a.m. – they still wanted to see the eclipse. The couple got in the bed and together they watched TV for some time. When it was about 11.03 p.m. the wife fell asleep. Her husband, however, was staying awake longer: Caroline had become somewhat frightening to Steven. What if she really was the one who did all this? But soon his love towards her gave him some positive thoughts: tomorrow they would be going back home and all would be fine. With these thoughts Steven was relaxed and he was able to sleep as well. But little did they know that the following night would be the worst of all they ever had – the real *phantasmagoria*!

9.

July 18th

It was 3.45 a.m. Up to this point Steven and Caroline had been sleeping in peace. There was perfect silence in the room. Through the window the full moon gave its light all over the room – illuminating the wall above the bed. Then, suddenly, this peaceful atmosphere began to break: the lock in the door began to bristle and shake – followed by a new silence. The door was slowly opening and there was a creak from the threshold – with no cause to be seen. There was the sound of steps before the door, then across the floor and finally at the window – and still nothing to be seen. But then a large, dark shadow cast itself on the wall. It was moving across it – like a spider in its web. The shadow stopped at the sleeping wife, covering her face all over. The thing causing this shadow stood right in front of the window, with its face turned towards her. Now her face began to look uneasy and her dream got a sinister transformation.

In her dream Caroline was standing in the hall of the cabin. Darkness was surrounding her and her heart was pounding very rapidly; on her retinas there were still the haunting images from the previous nights. On top was the one where the invisible figure had cut the mattress with scissors. By now she had seen it twice and it had begun the same way – standing in the dark hall and then hearing the cutting sounds coming from upstairs. This memory gave Caroline chills and she remained still in the darkness. She was shaking and trying to prepare herself for the upcoming sound. The terror was building itself up inside her chest. The wife was sure that horrible sound would come from the bedroom any time soon. But there was nothing to be heard, no sound at all. This made her more fringhtened, but she still kept on waiting the sound. A minute passed and another – still nothing. At that point Caroline's fear was partly turned to wondering since in the previous nights the sound had come almost instantly. Even though terror was still present, she decided to go to upstairs and look in the bedroom. Slowly she walked to the stairs and began to climb up. During this ascension she could feel how fear and terror began to grip her once more: by every step she could remember more clearly all the terrible experiences from the previous days – starting from the blood disappearing off the mattress and ending with the bloody figure in the mirror yesterday. These gruesome memories were devouring her soul – just like maggots do with a dead, rotting dog. However, she kept on ascending the stairs.

When Caroline had reached the bedroom door, she stopped and began to listen. The door was a bit open. She stood right at it and nervously tried to listen if there was anyone in the bedroom. She did hear some heavy breathing – as if someone was sleeping in the bed. Then it came to her that it might be her husband. This thought, however, didn't give her any comfort – there might still be others in the room. In an instant she was again thinking about the heinous shadow figure which given her terror during these days. Caroline also felt great worry for her husband who might be in terrible danger. So without further thinking she opened the door – quickly but gently – and stepped inside the bedroom.

Caroline was expecting to once again see the thing sitting on the bed and cutting the left mattress with scissors. What she saw was strange and not what she had expected: there were two persons – a man and a woman – laying on the bed. The woman was on the left mattress, sleeping heavily. The man was on the right one, but he was awake: he rubbed his hands together and looked at the sleeping woman every once in a while – he seemed to be pondering something and looked unhappy. Caroline was standing at the door, but he was paying no attention on her – apparently she was invisible to both of them. She was quite puzzled for what she saw, but still somewhat frightened. Her excitement, however, had calmed down since she hadn't seen the terrilbe things she had expected. But then Caroline looked these unknown people more closely and could feel her pulse rising once more: this was the very couple she had seen in the wedding photo – the husband Robert and his wife Suzan! She was looking at these two with fear and insecurity; she had no idea why she was seeing all this.

For some time Caroline was standing near the bedroom door, looking intently at the couple in the bed. Robert laid his right hand on his wife's left breast and began to rub it. Suzan, however, wasn't pleased with this: she removed her husband's hand off the breast and told him to sleep. Robert was seemingly frustrated by this. He then took hold of his wife's left arm, moved her hand in his pants and rubbed it against his cock. When Suzan saw what he was doing to her, she began to shake her left hand furiously and scratch with her polished fingernails: she gave Robert deep cuts all over his cock and balls, and he was screaming in pain. He let go of Suzan's left arm, leapt out of the bed and stood in the middle of the bedroom – with his crotch stained with blood all over. Suzan looked at Robert and began to slur insults at him: she called him with all sorts of disgusting names and then threatened to take him to divorce court – leaving him with nothing.

Caroline turned her eyes back towards Robert. But when she saw his face now, she was struck by terror: his face had become dark and there was a sinister look in his eyes – they were just burning with hatered and anger! It was then Caroline noticed his eyes were not fixed on his wife but on something else; he was looking intently towards the nightstand – and so did Caroline. There were a couple of objects on this table: the first one she noticed was a handbag – the very one she had found in the forest! Next to the handbag there also was a pair of scissors.

What happened next was something so horrible it made Caroline's blood become like ice: Robert took the scissors with his right hand, stepped next to his wife and lifted the blades above her head! Suzan screamed and she tried to escape, but her husband struck her head with his left fist – and she fell on her back unconciouss. But then Caroline leaped and attacked Robert – screaming and trying to stop him. But it was futile; no matter how much she screamed at him, beat him and kicked him, it didn't have any effect on him. So Caroline was forced to back out and look with terror how he was holding the scissors over his wife's left eye. At the very moment – it was 9.10 p.m. – the whole room became dark. Caroline ran to the window and looked outside: a lunar eclipse! And then – while she was still looking through the window – there were some horrible sounds in the darkness: cutting with scissors, slicing of flesh, moaning and groaning filled with pain and suffering! Caroline was filled with terror. She began to scream and weep in deaspair. Out of her subconciousness were flowing out all those macabre visions and horrible sounds of the previous days – and now they were taking over her mind! Her thoughts were now in total chaos and the only thing ruling over them was the fear with no mercy. Caroline went near the right corner of the window and knelt down in a field position – constantly shaking with terror. Finally those horrifying sounds made her to cover her ears and close her eyes as well. During the following moments – they felt like an eternity – her only companions were darkness, silence and what was inside her own head – an *inferno*!

10.
July 18th

Time went on for a moment, and another, even third. For all this time Caroline was unable to see or hear anything. Finally – since nothing was happening – she decided to open her ears and eyes. She removed her hands from over her ears – while shaking and preparing herself to hear something creepy. But there was nothing else but silence. However, she was too scared to open her eyes. She stood up groping around her and was leaning against the wall. Suddenly she heard a sound out of darkness: someone was breathing heavily again. It startled her since it was coming from the bed. However – even when terror was present – the first thought entering her mind was Steven sleeping in the bed. At the moment this was the nicest option and it stayed the topmost in her mind. Caroline was suggesting to herself the nightmare was already over and she would be able to go back to sleep with her lovely hudband. She was somewhat relaxed to such an extent she turned around and opened her eyes – expecting to see her beloved Steven again.

The sight facing her was hideous and familiar from the previous nights; she was once again looking at that gruesome figure who was sitting on the left mattress and cutting a hole with scissors at its lower-left corner. But this sight was the most creepy one: the thing cutting the mattress was now totally visible! Caroline was now able to be sure the figure sitting on the bed was a woman! Her hair was long and blonde, her skin was pale and full of black flecks. She was wearing a blue, blood-stained dress. Her face, however, wasn't visible – her head was bent forward and her long hair covered her face. Caroline was staring with horror how that bloody figure was once again cutting the mattress – followed by that dreadful sound:

CLIP!

CLIP!

This brought every horror vision back to her memory like a flash – and she was nearly blacked out by the terror. The woman sitting on the bed had finished cutting a perfect circle on the mattress. Then that thing took hold of the fabric and ripped it off: the mattress was left with a clear, round hole. Caroline lifted her eyes from it and fastened them at the unknown woman's head.

But then – all of a sudden – the thing lifted its head and uncovered the whole face: it was pale, wounded and blood-stained – and the left eye was missing. In an instant she realized it was the same figure she had seen in dreams and while being awake. That heinous face was grinning and staring her directly into the eyes. Her fear and terror became unbearable – unleashing a loud and desperate cry from her mouth. Caroline was screaming while that bloody woman was grinning at her. Then the nightmare was over, she woke up and found herself back in the bedroom.

Steven was sitting next to her and was trying to comfort his frightened loved one. Overcome with fear Caroline was weeping bitterly and embraced him with an uncontrolled passion. She then removed her nightshirt – showing her naked breasts. This act of hers got Steven very excited and his cock was erect in an instant. So they quickly took off their clothes, but they didn't go to bed. Instead, Caroline told Steven to lay down on the floor – and he did. His cock was hard and stiff – and shaking with excitement. His wife was walking around him with hands on her hips, fingering herself and teasing him with her wet pussy. So Steven decided to do the same to her: he took hold of his cock, rubbed and masturbated with it. After a while Caroline stopped and stood over Steven's face. She then knelt down and sat on his face – laying her wet pussy all over his face. She reached out toward his crotch, taking hold of his cock and began to suck it. And for both of them, this was the dirtiest and most perverted act they could think of. Caroline was sucking Steven's cock while he was licking her pussy. They had never done this before – and normally never would. But this cabin wasn't normal – and neither was Caroline or Steven. For some time they were able to keep going – and then both of them came: Caroline squirted her juice all over his face and Steven shot his cum all over her face. They both got up and looked at each other's eyes – feeling shame for their act. Caroline took a roll of paper towels and gave Steven some of them as well – without saying a word. They cleaned up their faces and put their clothes back on. The couple returned to bed and Steven turned off the light. After they got under the blanket, there was peace for a while. But then Caroline began sobbing – for fear, terror and shame – and Steven turned his face towards her.

He tried to comfort his wife by laying his hand on her head. Caroline was hysterical for her promiscuos acts; she was unable to understand how she could have done such perverted things! Steven tried to calm her by telling he wasn't able to compehend his own behavior either – and he promised her everything would be fine. Then Caroline began to tell him what she had seen in her dreams last night. This, however, made Steven angry, for he was tired of those stories. But as his wife just went on and on with it, he slapped her on the cheek and told her to shut up. This, in turn, got her furious and so full-blown arguing began between them. This, however, didn't last very long: it came to an abrupt end by the sound of the alarm clock.

11.

July 18th

Caroline and Steven looked at the clock: the time was 4.15 a.m. Suddenly the TV turned on by itself and began to make strange, whirling sounds. They looked at the TV screen, but only fuzzy static was displayed on it. Steven and his wife were staring the screen for a while. And then something terrible happened: a woman's face appeared on the screen! It was the very face Caroline had seen just a while ago! That grinning, blood-stained face with gore flowing out of the left, empty eyesocket! Pure terror got grip of Caroline and her husband as well. She was in a shock and told him this was the figure she had seen in her visions. Steven was feeling great fear and horror while looking at the hideous face – staring back at him. But then the screen went black: the TV turned itself off. They were both staring at it – both of them nervous and soaking wet with sweating. And it was then Caroline felt something strange: chilling coldness going over her whole body.

She turned her eyes to the outer side of the bed. What she then saw was this: there was a heavy shadow, slithering from the foot end of the bed and casting itself over her! The wife could feel how her fear and heartbeat were rising up. But then she noticed the weird behavior of her husband: he was sitting on the bed in horror and pointing at the wall behind her back. So she turned to look at the wall and was terrified: the dim moonlight shining through the window – the lunar eclipse was just about to be complete – cast a woman's shadow on the wall! It was the very same woman who had appeared in the horrible visions and on the TV screen! Caroline got off her own side and embraced her husband in fear. Now he really believed her story; there was no-one to be seen before the window, but the shadow showed it was there!

The couple was watching this sight in horror, when the bedroom was, suddenly, swallow by darkness; the eclipse was now perfect. The clock was showing the time 4.20 a.m. Steven quickly opened the nightstand drawer, took out a flashlight and turned it on. He pointed the beam of light towards the window – revealing a sight of terror: at the spot where the invisible thing stood, something was becoming visible! At first there was an obscure, dark figure with no details. But these features were appearing slowly and finally they were clearly to be seen. Caroline and Steven were shaking with fear: there before the window was now standing a bloody and pale woman, staring at them with her right eye – the only one. Caroline was terrified – more than ever before; she was able to clearly see that abhorrent thing, staring at them with a sinister grin on its face. Likewise Steven's eyes were fixed on the bloody woman in a blue dress, standing before the bedroom window – he was gasping for air. They were all totally still – the couple and the woman.

Suddenly the bloody woman began to move: she walked across the bedroom floor all the way to the door. Caroline and Steven were the frightened witnesses of all this. The dark figure grabbed the handle and opened the door. She then stepped to the staircase and began to move downstairs. The disturbed couple lost sight of the woman. Then the nervous Steven began talking to his wife – she was too scared to say anything. At first he apologized her for being offensive and

admitted she had been right all this time. Steven
decided they needed to leave this place – as soon as
possible, never to return. These words gave her comfort
and she agreed with him. Steven was then hurrying
Caroline to get dressed right away, since that hideous
thing might come back at any moment; they had no
idea what intentions the woman had – and absolutely
no willingness to stay and find out. They got dressed in
a hurry and then went to the open bedroom door. They
saw the unknown thing was nowhere to be seen. Steven
then moved himself to the staircase and began his
descending to the first floor. Caroline was following
right behind him – feeling great horror and fear; it was
as if her nightmares had become *incarnate*!

After reaching the end of the staircase, Steven's
heart began to pound in full power; he wasn't able to
see if the thing was in the hall or not. He was hesitating
for a while – but finally he dared to take a peek at the
hall: it seemed to be empty. After he told this to
Caroline, she also was able to step in the hall. Steven
turned the lights on – and now the hall seemed to be
even more empty than before. Then he went to the
cabinet and took out the gun he had hidden there. The
husband gave it to his wife – to have the chance to
defend herself against this unknown threat. Caroline
took the gun with her shaking hands. But then – all of a
sudden – she was startled by some strange, ticking
sound; it was right behind her back! Quickly she turned
around and saw something very odd: it was the sound
of the clock which was hanging on the wall – it had
somehow started working again! However, the way the
clock was working was quite unusual: its hands, which
had stopped at 9.10, began to move around its face in
an accelerated pace! The clock was moving forward

with a great speed – until the hands stopped excatly at 4.30: the present! A deep, rustic echo made its way out of the clock – making Caroline feel even more uncomfortable; her thoughts were ripped by the haunting insecurity of what was happening to her and his husband.

Steven tried to comfort her by telling it would be over soon – and Caroline told him she was ready to leave this horrible cabin for good. They started walking towards the hall door. She was going first with the gun in her hand; she was encouraged by the trust of her beloved husband to overcome the fear. Since the cabin hall was now lit, all they saw through the windows was darkness. Caroline had just arrived to the door and was reaching her hand towards the handle – and then she was blacked out! The cabin door was opened from the outside in a very aggressive way: it struck her forehead violently! She was knocked out cold and collapsed on the spot. So Caroline was unable to know anything of that dreadful horror her husband was now about to face all alone …

12.
July 18th

For about half an hour Caroline was laying on the floor unconciouss, but then she revived. When she opened her eyes, she was feeling an excruciating pain on her head. She was able to rise herself up to sit on the hall floor. It was then when she put down her right hand, it was met by something wet and soaked. The wife turned her eyes to see what it was: there was a large, wet trail – containing water, mud and blood – entering the cabin through the open door. Seeing this made Caroline gasp and she got on her feet quickly. She then followed the trail with her eyes: it entered through the door and slithered through the hall floor. And then she looked at the kitchen doorway – and was given a sight causing her to go white: there was a human hand in a puddle of blood! This gave her a vile suspicion and she ran to the kitchen door. When she got at it, she saw the whole kitchen floor – and was shocked by the gruesome sight: there was – on the floor, near the doorway – her dead husband laying in a blood puddle! His chest had been torn open, his lower jaw ripped off and both of his eyes pierced! The corpse was surrounded by a great amount of blood – mixed with water and mud. When she saw this terrible sight, she thought her heart had stopped; her beloved husband – with whom she had tried to have children so hard – had now been taken from her in the most vile manner! She fell down next to his dead body and began to cry bitterly. Her pain was now so insufferable, she felf like the whole reality was shattered to pieces.

Caroline was weeping over Steven's death – by pouring out endless tears. Then the hall clock echoed and frightened her. The clock echoed five times – and every single one of them felt like a gunshot through her heart. When the sounds had finally ceased and silence was back, she was standing at the kitchen door, facing the staircase. Despite her weeping she was able to see how the trail of blood, water and mud went to the stairs and then up upon them. So she was able to conclude the monster who had killed Steven would be there. But just as she had gone to the end with this thought, a sound was coming from the bedroom:

CLIP!

CLIP!

Hearing this gave Caroline deep chills; all the nightmares of the three previous nights were flowing from her subconciousness. She was recalling that creepy-looking thing sitting on the bed and cutting a hole in the mattress; its horrible, grinning face was still haunting in her mind. But the worst part was, however, that she was absolutely sure she was awake: everything she had seen in her dark nightmares would become reality. Her fear towards that thing and her grieving for Steven were mixed together, forming hatered. Caroline really wanted to kill the vile beast who had killed her beloved husband. She was still afraid for her own life, but her hatered for the thing was stronger: momentarily it gave her enough courage to go upstairs. Then she remembered the handgun she had been given by Steven. At first she assumed she had dropped it and it was now under the sofa. She knelt down and looked under the sofa: it wasn't there.

Caroline discovered the gun while she went past the kitchen and looked at her dead husband: Steven was holding it tight in his right hand! It seemed he had taken the gun and had tried to kill the thing – before it killed him instead. The wife was gasping while she knelt down to her dead husband and took the gun out of his hand. She then went out of the kitchen and checked the bullets of it: five were already fired and three were left. With these three bullets she walked to the stairs and began to ascend. And then – when she had taken a few steps – the dreadful sound came again:

CLIP!

CLIP!

Caroline got a bit startled, but didn't let it slow down her – she had decided not to lose her courage; based upon her dreams she was confident about what she would see in the bedroom. She walked the stairs hastily but carefully – they were covered with blood, mud and water. After she reached the top of the stairs and stood at the bedroom door – it was a bit open – she was met by a horrible stench; it was like the reeking of a rotten, maggot-infested meat. Caroline was feeling sick and she almost threw up. She, however, was determined to enter the bedroom. She took hold of the handle and slammed the door open. Then she quickly stepped inside the room and was pointing the gun towards the double bed.

What Caroline saw was basically the same as in her nightly visions: there was a dark figure sitting on the left-side mattress of the bed. It was cutting a hole near the lower-left corner of it, using the scissors taken out of the nightstand drawer. But what she wasn't expecting was its appearance: it sure looked somewhat like the dead bride Suzan – as Caroline was expecting – but quite faintly. It was grinning in a vile way. It was wearing a nightdress – a dark grey one, stained by mud and dripping water. Its skin was dark grey and covered with black spots. Its body was – from top to bottom – just skin and bones, muddy and wet. The things dark, grey hair was dripping water. But the most horrifying fact was it didn't have eyes at all! On its head were two empty holes where the eyes should have been. Caroline was staring – frozen by fear – at the dark thing, which was dripping mud and water. It was cutting the mattress with a pair of scissors – just like she had seen in her dreams. Now she was just standing and shaking – she didn't have any courage to move.

When the hideous thing had cut a perfect circle on the mattress, it took hold of it and ripped it off: there was now a large hole at the lower-left corner – Caroline had already seen all this in her dreams. But then the figure put its skeletal hand through the hole, reaching inside the mattress! For a while it was feeling around the insides – as if looking for something. But then, suddenly, it pulled out its hand – and there was something stuck between its fingers, something small and round. At first Caroline was unable to determine what it was, but after looking at it for a while she knew. She covered her mouth with her hands to suppress her scream! There was no doubt: it was an eyeball – a human eyeball inside the mattress! The thing brought the eye near its face and put it in an eyesocket – the left one. In an instant the thing let out a dreadful, inhuman screech. And then Caroline – who was hearing the screech, smelling the rotten stench and scared to death – was unable to take it any longer: she collapsed on the floor and gave out a huge vomit all around her.

Now the freak turned its hideous head and stared at her with its only eye and a vile grin on its face. Caroline got up from the floor and pointed the handgun at the thing. But then it rose up from the bed and began to come closer to her. She was horrified and was threatening it with the gun, telling it to stop. The thing wasn't paying any notice to her threats, but was still coming towards her. Caroline then fired a shot at it: the bullet struck the things chest, but it seemed to have no effect on it. She fired the thing with another bullet – this time it hit the left leg: still no effect. Finally she fired the third shot against the thing's forehead, but it was still coming to her; at this point it was so close to her it cut her right arm with the scissors. She felt burning pain in her arm and collapsed on the floor. Caroline was holding her bleeding arm and looked up: she saw the horrible beast standing before her, holding the bloody scissors with its right hand. She was looking at its hideous face and thought this would be her death. But then – when all hope seemed to ne lost – something very strange happened: the freak didn't touch her but it turned around, walked to the bedroom door and began to descend the stairs. In the middle of her fear Caroline was wondering what was going on. After the thing had gone down so it was no longer in sight, the wife followed it; she wanted to be sure if the thing was leaving. So she stepped to the staircase nervously and began to descend slowly. At the moment her mind was a total chaos; all the dreadful night visions had now become reality and Steven was laying dead. The horrible thing of her dreams had turned real – become flesh!

All these thoughts gave chills to Caroline, who had just reached the bottom of the stairs. She hadn't had time to think of anything else, when her eyes turned to the kitchen. The dead Steven was still laying there in the doorway – but then she saw something weird: the dark thing was standing in front of the kitchen table and was going through the handbag – the one found in the forest yesterday. Caroline was now standing at the bottom of the stairs, staring nervously at the gruesome figure. But after a while the thing suddenly took something out of the bag: the wedding photo of Robert and Suzan. Then it took the scissors and used them to cut a hole in the photo. Caroline was feeling disturbed seeing this, but soon she felt frightened: suddenly, the thing let out that terrible, inhuman schreech! After that the thing began to walk. At first she was startled when it walked out of the kitchen and was coming right towards her. However, it didn't pay any attention to her – the thing passed by her, went across the hall and out of the open door, disappearing into the darkness outside. Caroline stood still and was unable to move for terror. But after a while – when it was safe to assume the thing wasn't coming back – she went to the open door, closed and locked it. While she was returning from the door her eyes were wandering across the wet and muddy floor. Then she discovered something: it was the photo that freak had cut just a few moments ago. Caroline picked it up and looked at it – and she noticed something creepy: the hole was cut right where the head of the husband had been! So the photo was now showing the bride Suzan and her husband Robert – and he was now beheaded! After Caroline saw the photo, everything she had seen during the last days – the dreams, the visions and the experiences – seemed to her like the pieces of a puzzle; now she was able to put them together and see the whole picture ...

13.

July 18th

Caroline was convinced the thing really was the bride of the photo – Suzan – who had stayed at this cabin with her husband Robert ten years ago. But a gruesome act must have taken place here; she recalled all too well her vision of Robert attacking Suzan with a pair of scissors! Based upon her vision Caroline determined Robert had ended up killing his wife after they had been arguing with each other. After he killed her, he hid the body and claimed she had gone missing. The body had been hidden somewhere nearby – apparently it had been at the bottom of the lake; the dark figure had been dripping with mud and water, not to forget the hand which had grabbed Caroline by the foot in the lake!

Suddenly she came to realize what had begun these creepy events; all had started that very day she and her husband arrived to the cabin. What had happened first back then? Caroline remembered the scissors cutting a wound on her foot and blood spilling on the mattress. Then this blood had suddenly disappeared – with the odd and creepy sound of slurping. After this the dreams and visions of terror had begun. Then she remembered the mattress being cut in her dreams had been the very one where blood was spilled. And it had happened in real life this night – resulting with the thing taking an eyeball from inside the mattress and putting it into its eyesocket.

All of a sudden Caroline was able to understand the rest of events: when Robert had killed Suzan ten years ago, he had struck her left eye first. This had unplugged the left eyeball, which then had rolled through the hole and ended up inside the mattress. This eye had been a part of the bride – who was filled with sadness and hatered at her moment of death. The eyeball had been hidden inside the mattress for ten years – just like the rest of her body at the bottom of the lake. But a few days ago the blood spilled on the mattress had revived the eyeball – and her soul as well. At first it had been only spiritual and unable to hurt anyone. Therefore it needed to re-enter its body; this could only be done during a lunar eclipse, since the bloody killing had taken place during it.

Caroline then remembered she had encountered two very different beings in her visions: there had been the gruesome, grinning freak who had tormented her, but also the beautiful, sad woman who had helped her. She figured those two characters were the one and the same person (*ego*), but two opposite sides of it: the beaufiful woman was the pure and noble side (*superego*), which loved and wanted to forgive. On the other hand, the ugly thing was the evil and dark side (*id*) – full of hatered and thirsting for revenge. So Suzan's good and evil side had been fighting against each other, but the evil one had been more powerful. Therefore the good one had appeared to Caroline and revealed the truth. All of this had happened apparently because only she could stop the evil one – the hideous thing who had disappeared into the night just a while ago.

She then startled as she realized what was the meaning of all this: the bride Suzan – now as an undead – had set out to find her husband Robert in order to avenge her death to him. That's why the good side of Suzan had appeared to Caroline so she could stop this evil thing from happening. She also recalled this: when she had spoken with the agent yesterday, he had given her the husband's name and his hometown. Caroline decided to go there, find Robert and warn him before the undead Suzan would get her revenge. Then she was troubled, as she recalled her own husband laying dead at the kitchen. But her first priority at the moment was to make sure no more new deaths would come – Suzan was counting on her! Since there would be no-one coming to the cabin, she decided to leave Steven the way he was. She then took care of her own wounded arm, put on her outside clothing, took the car key and went out. She had with her Suzan's handbag and the items it contained. After closing and locking the cabin door she walked through the dark yard and arrived at the car. She stepped inside and tried to start it with the key – and she succeeded! So Caroline started her race against the time: to find the husband before his undead wife did! Or at least she thought so …

14.

July 21st

Three days had passed. Caroline had been driving a total of 24 hours, spent one night at a drive-in motel and had stopped to ask for info multiple times. She drove as in a peril straight toward the place where Robert was residing – even though she was concerned for his life, not her own. It was a long and desperate search, but finally she arrived to a small, shaggy-looking house. Caroline checked the address and concluded this was the place. After she had stopped and locked the car, she rushed to the front door through the yard – it was full of broken cars, bicycles and other metal junk. At the door she used the doorbell – but no answer came. She was getting nervous, and pushed the button the second time – the third – and the fourth. And then the sound of steps could be heard coming from the inside – followed by unlocking the door. The door was opened just a bit and Caroline heard the raspy and tired sound of a man; he was asking who she was and what she wanted. Caroline introduced herself and asked the man if was Robert – the one who had been married to Suzan. He was hesitating for a moment, but then told her he was the one – and asked again what she wanted of him. Caroline was looking around her nervously and told him she had a very important business. When she then asked Robert to let her in so she could talk to him, he wasn't willing to do so. For this Caroline lost her cool and told him it was about life and death. It was then the door fully opened and she saw a tired, shaggy man standing at the doorway. She could tell with certainty he was the husband in the photo; it was obvious, however, the years had taken a big part off that sorry-looking ruin of a man standing before her, smoking a cigarette and coughing. Robert invited her to come in and she did. He closed the door and locked it.

After closing the door he began directing her to the living room. While they were going, Caroline looked around her and saw some peculiar stuff there: a stack of unpaid bills, some empty bottles of liquor and beer, a few pornographic magazines, and some joints of weed. Then they came to the living room. Robert invited her to sit on an old armchair; Caroline sat on the chair and he got the couch. He was now asking her to tell him what she was doing here – and Caroline began to speak: at first she was insecure while asking Robert if he had been married to Suzan – and his answer was positive. Then she asked him if they had spent time at a certain cabin ten years ago. Now it took a longer time for Robert to answer, but he did admit Caroline was right – and his old cigarette had expired, so he took a new one and lit it. But when she asked him what had happened there ten years ago, he gave no answer; his appearance went pale and he began to act nervously.

When Caroline was asking the same question a second time, Robert got furious and told the same story she had heard before – about the young man stopping their car, knocking him out and the disappearace of his bride. He was nervous and told her he had said all this to the police and knew nothing else. Caroline cut his story short by calling him a liar. She told him everything she and her husband had seen and heard at the very same cabin – the blood-sucking mattress, her visions about the scissors, the undead bride seeking revenge and the others. She was interrupted by him – or his unhinged laughter, to be exact. Robert the told Caroline she was out of her mind – and kept on laughing. This made her angry and she told him to believe her – and he, in turn, said she was insane and seeing just delusions. It was then Caroline took the photo out of her pocket and gave it to him. After Robert had taken the photo and looked at it, he was laughing no more. Instead, he was sitting in total silence and his face became white as snow.

He was asking her where she got the photo. She told him it had been inside the handbag she had found by following her dream about Suzan. As a proof she took the handbag and put it on the table between her and Robert. It was then he put the photo on the table and asked her if she was a cop or in co-operation with the cops. Caroline denied she had anything to do with the police. She then asked him to believe her: she told him about her vision of him killing Suzan, how she had returned from the dead to get her revenge, and how Caroline had come to warn him before his undead wife reached him. This was all she was able to tell Robert; after hearing this he got very angry, rose up from the couch and told her to get out of here. Caroline refused and was begging him to believe – to which he responded he had done nothing and calling her a lunatic. Robert forced her out of the front door – and threatened her with the police if she came back to him. Then the furious man slammed the door shut behind him. Caroline began walking back to her car – she was angry and sad at the same time. Robert was looking through a window to be sure that crazy woman would leave. When he saw she went to her car, he left the window and went to get a bottle of beer from the kitchen.

Robert entered the kitchen and opened the fridge. It was then he noticed a strange, disgusting stench – just like the smell of rotten meat. He went through the fridge to see if the stench was coming from it. Nope, there was nothing rotten in there. So he took a bottle of beer, opened it and took a sip of it. As he was leaving the kitchen with the bottle, his feet got suddenly wet. Robert looked at the floor and was disturbed: there was a huge trail with blood, mud and water. He then looked to his left and saw the back door was open. The trail seemed to begin at the threshold and to continue through the entire hall. He then began to walk towards the back door – frightened and totally clueless of what was happening. And then – while he was walking towards the door – a figure dripping with blood and water stepped out of the living room – behind him, without being noticed.

At the same time Caroline was standing beside the car – feeling disappointed and about to leave. But as she was going to enter the car, she then noticed something weird: the trunk at the car's back was open. She went to check it and got terrified; the trunk floor was filled with the mixture of mud, water and blood! She also saw there was a puddle of that disgusting mess on the ground; there was a long trail of it – going all the way behind Robert's house. And then Caroline realized the horrible truth: the undead Suzan had been hiding in the car trunk this whole time – and she had brought the beast straight to its prey! She began to run and follow the trail – and she hoped to get there in time. She followed the trail of blood, water and mud to the back of the house.

In the meantime Robert had reached the back door and was checking the yard; there was no-one to be seen. But then Caroline appeared before his eyes and she stopped at some distance from him. Robert was looking at her – feeling both amazement and anger. And then she saw that thing – the undead Suzan – standing right behind her husband's back and holding a pair of scissors in the right hand! Caroline then began yelling there was danger behind him and started to run towards the back door. After Robert heard these words, he turned around right away – and everything went black to him: the undead hand struck the blade to the husband's chest – and all the way through his heart! Robert turned into as pale as snow and he dropped dead on the floor. Then Caroline reached the house, rushed through the doorway and slammed the thing with her right shoulder. The undead flew backwards and fell to the floor – striking the back of its skull: the left eyeball – the one hidden inside the mattress – popped out of its head, flew in the air and landed on the hallway floor. Caroline placed the eyeball under her shoe and crushed it to a bloody mess under the heel.

The undead Suzan began to moan and groan in a hideous way – with the body shaking and twisting all over. And finally it was over: the dark, bloody thing was now lying on the floor – with no life and the face twisted by suffering. Caroline was looking at the undead and saw it wouldn't rise anymore; the left eyeball – the only living part of it – was now dead. She was standing in the middle of the hallway covered with blood – between the husband and the bride of the wedding photo. Robert was right at the doorway with a pair of scissors plunged into his chest. Suzan was lying in the middle of the hall, covered with blood and mud. Caroline was looking at the two bodies and she felt a great pain in her heart. Was this the end? Was there nothing she could do anymore?

Then – all of a sudden – one thing came back to her mind – an object she had taken along with her without even thinking about it. So Caroline went into the living room, took the handbag off the table and checked inside it. Finally she found what she was looking for: the rosary beads belonging to Suzan. Caroline took the beads and placed them on the dead woman's chest – as her final gift for Suzan. Blood was running out of her chest: it covered the beads and the image of the crucified attached to them.

In an instant something totally unexpected came about: the blood-covered cross began to shine with bright light – filling the whole house with it! Caroline got scared and the reality seemed to become blurry. She fell down on the floor, losing her conciousness and falling into a state of deep unknown …

15.

July 8th

Caroline woke up; she was soaking wet of sweat and fear when she opened her eyes. At first she was looking all around her very nervously – expecting to see the corpses again. But what she then saw gave her huge amazement: Caroline was lying on a double bed in a bedroom! It was, however, not the bedroom where she and her husband had spent those horrible days: it was their very own bedroom at home! The clock was displaying the time 6.30 a.m. Caroline was looking around her wondering and she saw her lovely husband – her beloved Steven – sleeping next to her, safe and sound! It was then her heart was lightened and she felt comfortable to say: it was just a very realistic and disturbing nightmare! Caroline then thought she and her husband should find some nice place to spend their vacation in. She remembered the horrible cabin from her nightmare. Therefore she decided to tell Steven they were going to spend the vacation at sunny, southern beaches; she wouldn't go to a forest to be in solitude and loneliness. She was feeling peaceful and comforted. So she gave her husband a kiss on the cheek, laid her head on a pillow and fell asleep right away.

Caroline – now fast asleep – was unable to see the person who appeared in the bedroom: it was the dead bride Suzan! But now her form was very different than before: she was once again the beautiful, blonde-haired woman in her blue nightdress! She stepped carefully at Caroline's side of the bed. Suzan had a smile on her face and was looking at her sleeping – now with two eyes. Her lips were moving and giving out inaudible words of deep thankfulness for Caroline; she had been able to defeat her evil self and so had finally given her soul peace and rest; she had finally been able to forgive her husband Robert. Then Suzan stepped a little further – leaving Caroline and Steven sleeping in peace – and she disappeared from the room – from time into eternity.

FIN

The Tower of Iron

"Where am I? How did I get here?"

Mr. X had just woken up. He was laying on his back
and looking straight up. The foor on which he was cold,
hard and wet. After feeling it for a while Mr. X was
able to tell it was made of concrete; it was like one of
the floors of the industrial halls where he had been
working for many years. Mr. X determined he was
currently in a hall similar to them. He then looked up
and saw the ceiling across which great beams of metal
crossed – and it was like in an industrial hall.

Mr. X was able to see around him to some extent, since
the hall was illuminated by an unknown source. Even
so it was still quite dark there and Mr. X was unable to
see the walls of this hall. He got up and was able to get
on his feet.

At first Mr. X wanted to know what was the source of
the light illuminating the dark hall. After he had risen
up, he noticed the light was originating somewhere
behind him. Without further thinking Mr. X turned
around and looked at the direction the light was coming
from.

"What am I looking at?"

Mr. X saw something he found to be both frightening
and fascinating at the same time: there was a huge
tower in the middle of the hall – with the light shining
from its top! For some time Mr. X was observing it and
taking notes: the tower was about 2000 feet high and its

diameter about 300 feet. It was made entirely of rusty iron, covered by human blood and excrement. The tower was shaped like a pentagram and there was a single door at its base – with no windows or anything else. The tower Mr. X was now seeing before him was like this. For a long while he was staying still and was nervously thinking what he would do next.

"Do I have to get up the tower?"

Mr. X was walking towards the door he saw before him, at the base of the tower. He came to the door and stopped to see what was inside: the floor, the walls and the ceiling were covered with the same hideous mess as the tower's outside. At the opposite and of the floor there was an iron ladder to access the second one. At first Mr. X was totally unwilling to enter the tower, but finally his curiosity got the best of him. So Mr. X stepped inside and entered the first floor of the iron tower.

"Now I am trapped in this darkness!"

In a instant Mr. X heard the door closing behind him and he ended up in total darkness. Mr. X turned quickly back towards the door and tried to open it. But even though he put all his strength to work, the door didn't move an inch. So Mr. X figured out someone had captured him for some reason. This thought increased his pulse and gave him an uneasy feeling – not to mention the darkness surrounding him and the stench of blood and excrement floating in the air. Despite all this Mr. X was determined to go up the tower, since that was the only choice he had. He went to the ladder, took a firm hold of it and began to climb to the second floor of the tower.

"This place is a real hell!"

So Mr. X went on further, climbing the tower up and up. But this turned out to be much harder than he thought – and much more terrifying! Each of the floors was totally different than the others. Even their internal structure was uneven; the floor went up and down with no symmetry; it was sometimes level and sometimes not; at one point the floor was smooth, but at another it was covered with iron spikes. What made all this even worse was Mr. X's inability to see around him at all; so he was compelled to search around with his hands and feet as he was moving forward. During his desperate climb Mr. X got wounded, bruised and crushed many times, over and over again. Hunger and thirst began also troubling him – and were getting worse and worse as time passed. Finally Mr. X's strength was nearly all drained and he was about to give up – but then he saw some light at the top of the ladder!

"This place is a real paradise!"

After climbing up one more set of ladders Mr. X saw he had reached the top of the iron tower. First he noticed the top was all flat; its floor was brightly lighted up all over and this was the mysterious light he had seen from below.

Then Mr. X looked before him and saw a huge table in the middle of the top; it was rectangular – 80 feet long and 30 feet wide. There was a big armchair at the end of it – and no other seats. The table and the chair both were filled with ecquisite, ornamental engravings – all of them were overlaid with pure gold. On the table – right in front of the chair – there was a large set of different kinds of dining utensils: a big plate surrounded by forks, knives and spoons – all of them pure gold. For drinks there was a golden cup decorated with valuable gems. It the same way were made all the utensils used for serving food and drinks: platters, bowls, cups, pots and trays.

There was an abundant feast set on the table: juicy roast and steaks made of the best and chosen bulls, cows and lambs; tenderly deep-fried birds – chickens, ducks, geese, doves, quails and peacocks – and also their fried, boiled and poached eggs; the seasoning was all sorts of salt and pepper, rosemary and basil, thyme and cummin, dill and parsley, mint, vanilla and cinnamon; tasty and richly-flavored cheese – with just the right texture; fried salmon, eel, tuna, red herring, dolphin, great white shark, killer whale, oyster, clam, lobster, crab and coral; boiled and fried vegatables – potatoe, pea, cor, red and green pepper, carrot, asparagus, broccoli and cauliflower; many sauces of first class – with a lot of cream, butter, beer, wine and all sorts of spices, including weed; red wine made of the best and juiciest grapes with great skill and effort – it had ripened in the longest and the most optimal way to ensure its delicious flavor; for dessert there were many sorts of cakes, pies, eclairs, cream puffs, fruits, ice cream, sweets, chocolates, donuts and smoothies.

The feast looked and smelled such that Mr. X – tormented by hunger and thirst – nearly fainted; he was so amazed and delighted. That wonderful banquet reminded him of something he had heard at his local church many years ago. What he remembered was this:

*"And in this mountain shall the Lord of
hosts make unto all people a feast of fat things, a
feast of wines on the lees, of fat things full of
marrow, of wines on the lees well refined."*
(Isaiah 25:6)

With these words on his mind Mr. X was about to burst of joy: he had now arrived to the paradise where he would never be hungry or thirsty again! Mr. X ran to the table with joy and started to feast: he took large portions of all kinds of food, gobbled the whole plate and kept refilling it. He also emptied many bottles of wine – one for each plate of food. Mr. X was feeling himself happier than ever before; he was eating and drinking like there would be no tomorrow. Eventually he had to stop this – when he felt greatly sick and became severely intoxicated.

"This horror can't be real!"

It was then Mr. X was hearing a voice behind him; it was calling him by name. So he got up from the chair, turned and looked to the direction the voice was coming from. Then he saw something so horrible he almost got blacked out: the voice calling him belonged to a hideous-looking hag – a hunch-backed one – with scars and boils all over her skin and wearing filthy, stinking rags! There also was a large group of children – 13 in total – around that hag; their skin color was yellow-green and their bodies were morbidly deformed

– with bloated heads, swollen eyes, teeth growing out their fingertips and their twisted feet! When Mr. X saw this horrible herd before him, it was too much for his sore gut: his entire stomach content – all that delicious food and drink he had enjoyed a while ago – got vomited all over the tower top; it became a huge puddle spreading itself all around him.

When Mr. X had finally stopped his throwing up, the hag began to speak: she told to be the wife he had abandoned many years ago – and she was here for recompensation. As she lifted up her head – revealing her face – Mr. X got pale by terror: it really was his ex-wife he had left to die in the woods! Everything had started from a serious brain desease – a tumor of unknown nature – Mr. X's wife had fallen ill with. He had taken care of her many years. But as the desease spread, she got more hideous and finally lost her abilty to walk. It was then Mr. X had taken her to a lonely cabin in the woods, locked her inside and left the place – as she was creaming and cursing him. Since then Mr. X had heard nothing of his ex-wife; he assumed she was now dead and gone. So Mr. X thought the suffering was now over – that is, his own suffering.

However, the brain tumor caused the wife's body to go through an unexpected transformation; she was now able to give her negative emotions a physical, tangible form in a supernatural way – a real witch! Mr. X was terrified as he was told who these kids were: they were born of the hatered the ex-wife bore towards him! She had become pregnant by it multiple time – and had given birth to all of these "children of wrath"! They had built this hall and the iron tower five miles underground

– slow and steady, during these many years. Once the work was finished, the children tracked down Mr. X, knocked him out and took underground. As they reached the hall, the kids – by their mother's order – destroyed the passage to the surface, trapping themselves permanently down here. After this Mr. X was placed laying on the floor – where he woke up!

Mr. X was told by the witch this would be his home from now on until death. He was also told the children would protect their mother from him – and even if he somehow managed to kill all of them, there would still be no hope for him; they were buryed deep underground and no-one would come to his rescue. She then told Mr. X it was time for him to take his responsibility of their children; since she had become pregnant by her hate towards Mr. X, he was the real father of these kids! Then the hideous horde of deformed brood began to walk towards him – to give their beloved daddy a group hug!

Mr. X – after seeing and hearing all this – ran to the edge of the top and plunged himself off the tower – falling down into the dark abyss.

The Devil's Mirror

Prologue

A summer cabin, somewhere by the sea. It was midnight and the full moon was shining. A car arrived at the cabin, and a man wearing a black leather jacket stepped out. He opened the back door and took a package of brown paper out of the car. The figure then walked by the sand path to the cabin and used a key to open the door. All this time the man was looking around him very nervously and he seemed to be frightened.

He stepped inside the cabin, turned on the lights, put the package down, took off his jacket and put it hanging. The man then picked up the package, sat on the couch and ripped open the package: an ornamental antique mirror of ebony was inside it. It was a unique article, one of its kind, and looking quite unusual: the frame was decorated with human faces engraved all over it – they looked tormented, screaming and wailing over their suffering! But when he took the mirror out, something else came out as well: an old, tiny scroll of parchment fell on the floor and rolled under the couch – the man didn't notice this. After he had taken the mirror with his hands, he looked at it for a while. He then went to the wall opposite the couch, took off a picture hanging on it and replaced it with the mirror. The man stood before it for some time – looking at his own reflection.

Suddenly he was startled – like he had seen something creepy in the mirror. And then came the sound – a screech so terrifying and shattering he had to cover his ears; this lasted for about half a minute. But as the sound died down, all the lights went out – leaving the man in total darkness! He was still standing before the mirror – shaking all over and looking around him. Then his eyes met the reflection in the mirror – and he screamed; what he then saw was a horror out of this world! The scream was cut short; what he saw in the mirror came over him like a flood. This was followed by a total silence.

Then, suddenly, another sound was heard in the cabin: it was as if someone was *scratching* wood! This lasted for some time – and came to a sudden end. After the sound had stopped, the lights went back on. The mirror was still hanging on the wall, but something was different about it: there was a new face – a screaming one – engraved on its ebony frame, bearing a striking resemblance to the man who had screamed just a while ago!

The Eve of Hell

Many years had passed since that fateful night. And then another car drove along the road to the cabin; the driver was a young man – a college student, about 20 years old – named Mike. He was in a perky and happy mood; the spring break had just begun, so he had rented a nice place for him and his friends to have a party. For the occasion Mike had filled the trunk with booze, pot and other kinds of necessities. In particular he was looking forward to see some of the chicks there – especially Cindy and Megan, the hot double-D twins. While his thoughts were focused on their voluptous bosoms, Mike didn't notice he was being watched: a strange, dark figure standing next to an oak tree by the road was looking at his driving – and as he passed by, stepped into the thick woods.

The car arrived to the cabin and stopped. Mike stepped out, opened the trunk and took the stuff he had loaded the car with. He then locked the car and began walking to the cabin door by the sand-covered path. After Mike got there, he put the stuff down, took out the cabin key and used it to open the door. He opened the door slowly and went inside. He checked through the cabin – and everything seemed to be in a good, clean order; nothing out of the ordinary.

Mike picked up the party stuff from off the terrace and he brought them in. He then started to unpack the bags he had brought: the beer, the booze and the snacks got stored in the fridge, the pot was put under the couch as a special surprise. Mike was whisteling all this time – without any worries, whatsoever. When he had finished unpacking, it was about 6.30 p.m. It was then Mike noticed something he hadn't paid any attention to before: an antique mirror with a frame of ebony. Mike went before it and tried to look at his reflection. The mirror, however, was covered with a thick layer of dust and filth, and he was unable to see through it. He then looked at the frame and saw the twisted, tortured faces engraved all over it. Mike thought this was revolting and whoever was the designer of this had a terrible artistic taste! He, however, decided to let it hang on the wall; it might give Cindy and Megan a nice fright – and him a nice threesome!

There was still a plenty of time before the guys and the girls would arrive; they would start at half over midnight and party all the way until dawn! So Mike decided to go for a swim, have a nice walk in the nearby forest and eat the dinner he had brought. He then decided to get some sleep before the party started. Mike went to the bedroom, fell on the comfy bed and began to snooze. The mirror, however, wasn't sleeping – in fact, it had just woken up!

The Demonic Awakening

Mike slept for a few hours. As the sun went down, the full moon began to rule the night – and it was more bright than usual. There was a deep silence all over the cabin. Up to this point Mike had been sleeping in peace. There was a digital clock on the nightstand – and the time was 0.00, excatly midnight. Then the silence was broken by a weird, creepy sound – the sound of *scratches*! Mike then opened this eyes just a bit. But when he heard that sound again and more louder, he got scared and opened the eyes in full. Mike got up and sat on the bed. He then began to listen – being silent and perfectly still. After a short while the sound came again – just like the *scratching* of wood! Now Mike got very nervous and was looking around him in terror. But then he thought of something that calmed him down; it was just the guys and the girls playing a nice, little prank on him! They had probably arrived early and when they saw him sleeping, decided to scare him for fun. Mike began laughing and calling his mates loudly, giving them his compliments for a good joke. But there was no answer – just the deep silence! So Mike got out of bed, went to the door and turned the lights on.

He was standing at the door and took hold of the handle. Then the sound was there again – the scratching – and it startled him. When there was silence again, Mike began to open the door very carefully and in silence. When the door was open enough, he reached his hand to the switch and turned the hall lights on. He then kept opening the door until it was fully open. After that Mike stood still for some time; he was looking around him and observing the hall. There was, however, no-one to be seen. In an instant the loud scratching was heard again and he got scared. Mike turned his head and looked all over the room – even quicker than before – but there was still nothing there.

Now he began to feel really uncomfortable; he definitely had no idea what was causing the sound. So Mike began walking silently from the door towards the couch placed on the opposite side – while keeping his eyes directed to the kitchen door. When he got to the couch, the kitchen doorway was fully visible. But still there was nothing. Then he turned around and looked at the couch behind him. Out of curiosity he decided to check under it – there might be a mouse or a rat scratching the floor! So Mike knelt down, bowed his head against the floor and looked under the couch. What he saw was not what he had been expecting: there was a tiny scroll under the couch! Mike reached his hand and took it from its hiding place. When he was holding the scroll, he saw it seemed to be old and made of parchment. He put it inside his pocket – in order to better examine it later.

And then – with no expecting – Mike heard the scratching coming right behind him! This time, however, it didn't stop but went on and on. He was frightened and turned quickly around to see what was making the sound. And the cause of the scratching was revealed to him: it was that creepy-looking mirror hanging on the wall – every time the scratching was heard, the mirror was moving by itself on the wall!

This sight filled Mike with terror and anxiety. But he was still able to control himself so he was able to examine the mirror more closely. He began to walk to the mirror very closely – while the scratching still continued. And when he had stepped right before the mirror, the sound stopped suddenly and there was silence. Mike looked around him, but there was still nothing special to see. So he turned his face back towards the mirror and he tried to see his own reflection on it. But the mirror was so covered with dust and dirt he was unable to do so. He went to the kitchen, took a cleaning towel and soaked it in water. He then took a bottle of cleaner, poured it on the towel and went back to the mirror. Mike scrubbed the mirror with some force and was able to make it bright; he was able to see his own reflection clearly. He stood before the mirror for a while, observing his reflection on its clean surface.

But then there was an ear-shattering screech in the room; Mike was startled by this and he covered his ears since the noise was so terrible. Suddenly it stopped and all the lights went out. He was now standing right in front of the mirror – surrounded by darkness and deathly silence. Full of fear and terror he looked all around him, but there was no-one in the dark room.

Mike turned his eyes back to the mirror without thinking about it – expecting to see his own reflection. Then he was met by a horrible sight: it wasn't his own image, but a hideous, demonic abomination looking at him from the dark depths of the mirror! The shock was so great Mike fell backwards to the floor and began to gasp. He was able to see how two bloody, death-pale hands reached out of the mirror and were furiously waving all around. Then Mike got up and he began to back off from the mirror. After a while the hands were pulled back into the mirror. Mike then saw another creepy thing; some kind of thick, black sludge – like tar or pitch – had began to come out of the mirror; it went down the wall and ended up on the floor – forming a big puddle of sludge. When the puddle was about eight feet wide, this flowing stopped. At that very moment Mike got a terrfying surprise; the demonic hands came up from the puddle and took hold of the edge of it. Then the freak lifted its ugly head out of the puddle! Mike was paralyzed when he saw the demon was coming out of the puddle! It stepped inside the room and stood in front of Mike. A giant cry came out of his mouth. And he then saw it – a great cry for help went on and on – that the thing was coming closer to him!

The Reflection of Death

The demonic reflection was walking slowly towards him; it had huge eyeballs bulging out of its head and a big, red tongue came out of its mouth, slithering to all directions. The freak was constantly making a creepy, growling sound. Mike's thoughts were overtaken by fear and terror, and he desperately tried to escape. He went back on and on, but the demon was approaching him all the more. When Mike had reached the bedroom door and tried to enter it, this is what happened: when the thing pointed at the door with its hand and clenched its fist, the door was instantly slammed shut and locked by itself. This scared Mike and he tried to open the door – but it was futile. And the creep kept on coming closer, so he had to go behind the coatrack. The reflection stepped to the other side and was ready to strike with its sharp claws. But then Mike noticed an iron pitchfork near the fireplace. Just before the demon was able to attack, he took the pitchfork and stabbed it through the freak's chest. It gave out a howl and fell down on the floor.

Mike stood still and waited for some time. After he was confident the thing was dead, he used the chance and ran to the kitchen. There he reached for the phone on the table, and dialed 911. To his horror Mike then noticed the phone was totally dead. And then – all of a sudden – he heard a sound from the mirror room; terrible growling and the sound of stepping! Then he reached for the kitchen sink and took out a butcher knife from the drawer. Next Mike turned around and faced the kitchen door – pointing the knife at it. Just then the demonic head appeared to the doorway and the horrible thing was slumping slowly into the kitchen. Mike tried to threaten the freak with the knife, but it didn't stop and just kept coming closer to him. Then he lifted up the knife and tossed it right towards the freak; the knife struck the left arm and sunk into it. In an instant Mike felt a piercing pain in his right arm. He took a look at it and saw a deep, bleeding wound on it. The mirror monster, however, was totally unhurt. The thing took hold of the knife with its right hand and pulled it out of the left arm – causing Mike an excruciating pain – and dropped it to the floor. Then the reflection stepped right to him, took hold of him by the throat and struck him against the wall. Mike was unable to set himself free and he was nearly helpless at the moment. The freak lifted up its right hand with sharp claws and it struck Mike's left wrist with its full might: the claws sunk into the flesh, cutting the veins and sinews like razorblades! Mike's left hand was cut off at the wrist and blood started to gush out of it. He cried for the enormous anount of pain, while the demon was laughing diabolically and waving the cut-off hand before his face. Then the freak bit off the fingers of the hand, and began to crunch them in a hideous manner. At the same time Mike was suffering a terrible pain and was trying to stop the bleeding of his wrist.

Then he saw something: there was a small shelf on the wall at his right side – and a flashlight on it. While the creep was still eating his left hand, Mike was able to grab the flashlight with his right hand. Then the thing was done eating his left hand and was preparing to strike his head. But then Mike was able to turn on the light and he pointed it right at the demon's eyes. The reflection let go right away and it backed off with a horrible scream. Mike was wondering this greatly. He then placed the flashlight on the table so it right at the demon. This gave him time to go to the drawer, get some bandages and stop the blood flowing from his wrist. When Mike had bound the wound, he turned and saw something weird; the thing howling in pain began to vomit the black sludge, covering itself with it. Then the black blob collapsed to the floor, dissolved and evaporated to thin air; no trace of the goo was left on the floor – or the demon itself! Mike entered the hall and saw it was totally emply. Now he dared to calm down a bit and sat on the couch. After he had sat down, he saw some blood dripping through the bandage. So she tried to find a handkerchief from his pocket, but instead he found something else: the old, tiny scroll from under the couch!

The Evil Mirror

Mike took the scroll and opened it. He sat on the couch and looked inside it; the scroll was old and brownish, but he was still able to read it. The content was as follows:

My dear friend,

When thou readest this letter I be already gone. Don't thou feel bad for my soul but in order to save thy own and that of the others thou must read this letter. I made a terrible mistake when I started studying that old antique mirror thou foundst from thy attic. I found out the truth about the mirror but it was already too late. It was created by a satanic cult in England during the dark ages. They worshipped the devil and tried to open a doorway to the otherworld so that the powers of darkness would devour our world. The sign of the cult

symbolized the evil mirror which was created by their hierophants. It was a gate to hell. And it is this mirror. Once the mirror was created, the hierophants wrote instructions of how to use it as a hell-gate. After a long research I finally managed to learn those instructions. According to the writings, first of all it must be a night of full moon to make it possible. Then thou must standest before the mirror and starest thy reflection to the eyes for some time. If all this is correct, a demon from hell will be able to possess thy reflection and come to this world. But there is also another part of the curse which must be fullfilled by the demon in order to stay in this world permanently. It must kill the person who summoned it and then thy flesh consume. I was insane when I decided to try the ritual and unleash one of the demons. We have to make sure none of those hideous things will ever get to this world again . No man will be able to kill them because they are protected by a dark spell. But there is a way of how to get rid of the demons which have made their way into this world and close the gate of hell for good. In order to make it happen thou mustest follow these instructions ...

After Mike had read the text this far, his examination was suddenly interrupted by the sound of the opening door. He was startled by this and he expected to see the demon once again. But it wasn't the freak he expected; instead, he saw Cindy and Megan rushing inside the cabin! They wore white mini-skirts and red crop-tops, revealing their bouncing D-cup boobs! The hot twins were followed by the other friends who had come for the party; there was a total of 15 persons inside the cabin now!

When Mike saw his friends arriving, he thought his heart was going to stop. Normally he would have been more than happy to see them, but this was not the case: there was a blood-thirsty demon on the loose, ready to kill and devour all of them! Mike was so overcome with fear and stress he ran to his friends and started to yell them to get the hell out of this place. Cindy and Megan were the most confused of them all – what on earth was wrong with the Magic-Mike – this was the nickname he had gotten for his amazing performance in bed. But then Mike told he had released a demon from hell and it had devoured his left hand – and he showed his bandaged arm to his friends. When they heard this, they laughed so hard they were about to burst; they thought this was the funniest thing Mike had ever come up with! When Mike saw how they were laughing, he thought what he had just said and felt embarrassed; the things he had just let out of his mouth sounded very ridiculous when spoken out loud – there was no blaming Cindy, Megan and others for laughing at that! But the demon lurking here was real, Mike knew it.

The girls and the guys took out the drinks, pot and other supplies – and they got the party started! Mike was trying to keep his head cool and calm – scream and panic would get him nowhere. He was watching around him. On the right Tom, Brad, and Nick were setting up the ultimate pot inhaler in order to get stoned like never before. And on the left were the double-D twins with Lisa, Karen and Heather mixing up the party cocktail according to their secret girls fraternity recepie. In the front Rick, Mick and Dick were having a nice barbeque with steaks, hot dogs and chicken wings. And on the back – last but not least – were Tracy, Molly and Katy talking about their sex toys and presenting the latest models to each other. Tonight they would have a good time – or get their money back!

While Mike was keeping an eye on everyone else, he saw through the cabin window to the yard. What he saw made his blood run cold: the demon was back and it stood just outside the cabin! Mike could tell it was now extremely furious; its eyes and mouth glowed like red, burning coals!

For a while Mike was totally clueless of what he should do now. But then he remembered something: the scroll had said the demon would have to devour the flesh of the person whose reflection it had posessed – so in this case that would be Mike himself! This would mean the freak was after only him and nobody else. So if Mike could keep a long enough distance between himself and all the others, his friends would not be in danger. But how that could be done? He thought for a minute and then an idea struck him! He spoke out loud to his friends and gave an important announcement: he would go to the guest room of the cabin – about 200 feet from it – in order to make preparations for the final surprise. His friends were very excited about this and promised not to sneak behind him.

With haste Mike took the flashlight and ran to the door of the cabin. He opened it, stepped outside and closed the door – locking it behind him. The demon was still outside and was approaching him slowly but steadily. So Mike began to run quickly from the porch towards the guest room. While he was running a dark figure was looking at him and the mirror demon from behind a nearby tree. Mike got to the guest room in no time. Then he turned and looked behind him – and he was terrified: the freak was much closer to him than he had thought – just about 10 feet away! It had already lifted up both of its clawed hands and was ready to strike him! Mike, however, knew what to do: he turned on the flashlight and directed it right at the demon's face. The thing screamed and covered its eyes with its hands. Then it covered itself once again with the black sludge, dissoved and evaporated – just like it had done before. Mike thought it would take a while for the thing to re- generate itself, so he went to the guest room door. He took the key out of his pocket and tried to place it in the keyhole. This, however, took him some time since he got nervous. He then looked around him nervously, but finally he got the door open. Right away he entered the guest room, slammed the door shut and turned on the lights.

Mike was soaking wet with fear. He tried the other door in the guest room. It opened and he turned on the lights – it was the bathroom of the cabin. He saw there was a security bolt on the door leading to the bathroom from the outside – and he locked it right away. After this Mike returned to the guest room and closed the door. He sat on the sofa and was soaking wet with sweat. After he had calmed down for a while, he took out the scroll he had put back inside his pocket. He decided to read it all the way to the end – in the hope of finding some way to slay the demon and save his friends. So he kept on reading the scroll, and the rest of it was like this:

There is only one way to break the curse. The mirror has to be broken! After that the spell is broken and the beast will go staight back to hell. I'm unable to do that because I have been trapped to the dining room where I'm writting this letter. I have time just to write this letter and send it off before the demon catches me. When thou get this letter, goeth to my house. The demon might still be there so be careful. I won't be there but thou mustst take that macabre mirror with thou. It's still hanging on the wall of my working room.

My friend, thou destroyest that evil mirror! It's the only way thou can save the souls of mine and of the other victims of the mirror and close the gate forever. Goodbye!

Thy friend,
R. W.

The Shadow of Death

After reading the rest of the scroll Mike remained seated for a while, pondering what all this meant. It was told in the text the mirror was a gateway between the world of humans and the world of demons. One of these freaks had possessed his reflection in order to enter the human world. All it had to do now was to kill the person who had woken it up. But it was impossible for a human to kill the demon directly. However, there was a way to stop it: by breaking the mirror the demon would be sent back to hell and the gateway would be closed. So Mike began to think how to trick the hideous thing and break the mirror. Suddenly he realized he had no idea where the freak was right now. He rushed to the window and looked outside: there was just darkness to be seen.

Suddenly Mike heard the sound of knocking at the door. He got anxious and went to the door, asking who it was. The voices of the twins Cindy and Megan were coming from behind the door. They asked Mike to open it so they could show him something very important. Mike opened the door, the girls went inside and he closed it. After he got the door shut he turned and asked what was it the girls wanted to show him. The sisters looked at each other, winked and began the show: they took off their shirts and removed their skirts – after which they also removed the bras and panties. Cindy and Megan were now just in the way Mike had wanted – totally naked and their big boobs bouncing joyfully. He was, however, so overtaken by all the excitement and the confusion he felt dizzy and fell backwards on the bed. The twins were a bit puzzled over this kind of reaction, but soon their interest was drawn by something else: his cock had become so stiff and hot it burst right through his shorts! Megan was the first who wanted to try riding it: she placed her wet pussy over the cock, put its top gently against the lips and sat down on it. Megan could feel the hot and stiff cock sliding inside her pussy and she moaned with pleasure. She began to ride the cock like a cowgirl, moving her hips up and down over it. Megan could feel how she and Mike were both about to come. Then they both came: Megan got a huge orgasm as Mike's cock filled her pussy with hot cum. So she got up and laid down next to him – with cum dripping out of her pussy. Her sister Cindy was not happy and she complained he would not have strength anymore. But in his dizziness Mike told her to try and see he would have all the strength she could possibly want. So also Cindy got laid with Mike. Her technique, however, was a bit different than her sister's; Cindy got over the cock – still hot and stiff – placed her pussy over it and let it slide very gently inside her. Then she let it stay inside her pussy for a while; she remained sitting on Mike, and her hips were tightly against his. Then she began to rotate her hips all around in a circular motion, so she could feel the cock all over her pussy. And then she came – just like her sister Megan; the hot cum from Mike's cock filled her whole pussy and gave her a massive orgasm. So she pulled the cock out and with her cum-dripping pussy laid herself down on the bed. The twins were amazed how he was able to give both of them an orgasm – and his cock was still hot and stiff! Cindy and Megan knew he was known as Magic-Mike, but this was just over the top!

After a while Mike came to his senses and he jumped up from the bed. He told Megan and Cindy to get dressed and get out of here. The naked twins, however, were quite giggling while they saw his shorts. So Mike looked down and saw the hole on the front side. He was embarrassed and changed his pants. Cindy and Megan also put on their clothes and they were quite pleased with Magic-Mike. He then asked the twins what kind of protection they had just used. The girls answered that sex had been unprotected, and he might have gotten them pregnant. This gave Mike quite an alarm, but the twins told him they would get the babies aborted so he could just calm gown. In addition they said they never used protection during sex and had a lot of abortions behind them – and they had found great pleasure in these abortions! When Mike heard this, his picture of Cindy and Megan was permanenttly shattered; the twins were indeed beautiful on the outside, but truly ugly on the inside. He didn't want to see them ever again.

Suddenly there was a hissing sound behind all of them. Everyone turned around and looked – there was no-one behind them. But then the lights went out. Mike took the flashlight in his hand and turned it on. He went through the dressing room and the bathroom, but there was no-one to be seen. So he went to the sofa and sat down on it.

Mike was sitting still and quiet, and was concentrated on listening. Cindy and Megan were also silent, but after a while they asked him what was going on. He told them the same story as before, but this time they didn't laugh at all. Cindy said the joke was old by now.

Megan agreed with her sister and with contempt stated the demons were just a figment of human imagination.

Since they were talking to each other none of them paid attention to what was happening in the darkest corner of the room; out of the shadows were reaching out two pale hands with sharp claws! They moved forward and were now just behind the double-D twins, reaching out to their necks. And then it happened: the claws sliced open the throats of both Cindy and Megan – causing their blood to gush out! The twins dropped dead on the floor.

Mike was terrified and looked at the floor: both Cindy and Megan were now lying in a puddle of their own blood! He then looked at the corner and was paralyzed with fear: the demon was now standing right there in the shadows! Its long tongue came out and licked the faces of the dead Cindy and Megan. This caused Mike to cry out in terror and to fall backwards on the sofa. While he was there shaking, the freak was approaching him all the time. Finally it reached Mike who was shaking and writhing by horror and disgust. At the moment Mike was fully worn out and thought death would come to him now. The freak had its giant maw opened and its breath smelled horrible. The demon's mouth was full of teeth – like scalpels and other surgical knives – which were about to bite his head off.

Mike was horrified and he groped the sofa with his right hand. But then his hand touched an object which he raised before his eyes: it was the flashlight! The demon was now so close he had only a few seconds left. So he lit the light and beamed the freak's eyes: it howled and collapsed to the floor. Mike kept pointing it with the light until it was once again covered with the sludge and disappeared from the room. By now Mike knew the thing was gone only for a short time. He also knew that until he was dead it would never stop. He decided to try to expell the demon by using the instructions of the scroll. Then Mike looked around the room for some tools or items he could use to break the mirror. In the darkest corner he found a tool box and opened it. He noticed a hammer and decided it was just the right tool, so he took it.

Mike opened the door very carefully and he went outside. His goal was to move back to the cabin in silence; since the demonic reflection cound be lurking anywhere, Mike was almost crushed by his fear. But finally he reached the main door of the cabin, took out the key and opened the door.

The Gateway of Hell

After Mike opened the door, he was met with the most gruesome sight ever: the cabin's floor, walls and ceiling were all covered with blood! His friends were all over the place – in tiny pieces! There was gore, intestines, corpses sliced wide open and cut-out heads everywhere in the cabin. Mike was shocked by what he saw. He had zero doubt the demon had killed all his friends. He began to walk through the room – avoiding blood, guts and bodies as well as he could.

Mike reached the demonic mirror and stopped right in front of it. There it was: the gateway between this world and the otherworld, and he had to break it. He observed its ebony frame and noticed there were plenty new faces engraved on it. At first he was surprised by this weird phenomenon, but soon it became a sight of horror: when he took a closer look at these screaming and suffering faces, he realized they were all his friends! The ones he first recognized were Cindy and Megan; it was quite easy since their D-cup boobs were also engraved on the frame! Mike gripped the hammer in his hand and this gave him some courage. He stepped close to the mirror and was getting ready to strike with the hammer. For a while Mike hesitated, but then he wielded the hammer and struck the mirror right in the middle. He gave out a sigh of relief. But he was disturbed when he saw the result: the mirror was totally unharmed – without even a single scratch on its surfce! Mike was horrified when he realized it might be impossible for him to break the mirror. Then he would be unable to save the souls of the victims – his and all the others' – from this terrible beast from hell! Mike had no idea how he could break the mirror and his mind was filled with despair. So he walked from the mirror to a wicker chair in the room. He was feeling very tired and so he sat down on the chair – resting his head against the back of it.

Mike had hardly sat down when a terrible thing happened to him; two pale hands reached out from behind the chair – sinking their sharp claws in his cheeks! He felt burning pain and screamed of agony. He tried to get free, but the hands held him in place. Then he looked right above him and was horrified; the terrible face was above him, and it dripped gore on his face! Mike was wailing of pain and disgust. Then he made a desperate attempt of escape; he pushed his head forward with all his power; the claws did mutilate his face quite a lot – causing him excruciating pain – but finally the thing lost its grip and Mike fell on the floor. For a moment he was lying and writhing on the floor due to the pain, but then he got up. Mike grabbed the flashlight from the floor and turned it on. He beamed the chair with it, but the demon was nowhere to be seen. So when nothing was happening, he began to approach the chair. When he was right before the chair, he bent over it and beamed behind it. Since nothing came out, Mike dared to look behind it: the demon was gone once again and it would be just a matter of time until it attacked.

In an instant Mike heard a hissing sound behind him and turned around. The sight was horrible: the demon was right before his face – staring at him with its big, bulking eyeballs! He reached out for the flaslight but the thing was quicker: it struck his right hand with its sharp claws, and so Mike dropped the flashlight on the floor – and it got smashed and broken apart! Then the demon punched him in the gut, causing him to cry for pain. The freak took hold of his throat, turned around and then slammed him against the wall with the mirror. Mike's head was right in front of the mirror and he was holding his sore gut with his only hand. The demon was holding his throat so tight he almost got suffocated. Mike then looked at the thing and was startled; it was ready to split his skull wide open! The freak was holding its right hand horizontally, right at the height of his forehead; it was pulled back just like an archer does with an arrow! The thing was about the strike him with its claws at full strength. Mike was shaking like a maniac and thought this was the end. And then – all of a sudden – the demon launched its claws toward Mike's forehead. But he was able to bend his head to the left just so the claws missed his head – scratching just his right temple. Then the wall was powerfully shaken and a loud screech was let out by the demon. It let go of Mike and he collapsed on the floor.

However, Mike didn't stay on that spot; he crawled away from the demon which was still standing in front of the mirror. Then he looked at it again and was amazed; it was before the mirror totally frozen – with its claws piercing the mirror's surface and having made deep cracks on it. Mike was looking at this weird spectacle. But then a dark, thick smoke started flowing out of the mirror through the cracks. It swallowed the freak all over and then it got sucked back into the mirror. In an instant the smoke was totally gone – and so was the demon!

Mike was filled with the feelings of joy, wonder and fear. He got up off the floor and looked at the broken mirror. Mike was feeling relief: the mirror was broken, the freak was gone and the gareway of hell was closed. But then he looked around him and saw all his dead friends. This caused him to sit down and weep bitterly. Mike did this for quite a while. After he finished sobbing, he lifted his head and looked towards the front door – and got scared: a dark-dressed man was standing at the open door! He stepped inside, went to the mirror and took it off the wall. Mike was unable to see the stranger's face – his hat and uplifted collar were hiding it – but when he was taking the mirror, his right arm was revealed; there was a mark on it – like a burned mark – shaped like this:

Mike knew this symbol: it was the sign of the cult which had created that evil mirror centuries ago! Very quietly he picked up the hammer and sneaked behind the dark man – trying to knock him out. But when he was about to strike the man turned around, raised his hand and sent Mike flying through the room. The back of his head hit the wall of the cabin – and everything went black.

Epilogue

Mike woke up and opened his eyes. He could feel quite a pain on his head – especially on its back. He could also feel something soft under him – a bed! Then he noticed it wasn't just any bed: it was a hospital bed – and that was the place where he was now! He also noticed his head and upper body were covered with bandages. Mike could feel his right hand and saw it as well. He was also able to feel his left hand – the one that had been cut off. This was no surprise to him since he had read about a phenomenon called "the ghost pain" occuring to people with lost body parts. He, however, lifted up his left arm and looked at it; his left hand was back there again – as healthy as ever! Mike didn't know what to say – all this seemed too good to be true. He then decided to pinch himself and he did it; this was not a dream!

Suddenly there was a knock at the door of his room. Mike got a little startled, but he invited the one knocking to come in. The door opened and he was baffled at what he saw: it was the double-D twins Cindy and Megan in their hot summer outfits! They had brought a gift with them: a big package made of brown wrapping paper. They placed it on the table and went to Mike's bed. He still couldn't believe his eyes, asking the girls if they were really there. The twins smiled at him, lifted up his hands – Megan the left one, Cindy the right – and put these just between their boobs. Mike got excited and his little-Mike turned to the big-Mike. The girls saw this and got naked in no time. When Mike asked them about protection, Cindy told him they always used the pills – and Megan agreed. So Mike was relieved and he gave the girls what they wanted – his magic cock! They had quite a party for half an hour. After they were satisfied, Cindy and Megan got dressed, kissed Mike goodbye and were about to leave. He then asked the girls what was in that package, but they didn't know; it was given by a strange man who wanted to give Mike a special gift, something "to reflect his true self". So it was.

Mike was alone in the room. He was dead, stone cold.

Limbo

Mr. Y was lying unconcious on the floor. He then revived and noticed he was in the middle of darkness. He looked around him, but he was unable to see anything – except the seemingly neverending darkness.

Suddenly Mr. Y saw that a small light appeared in the darkness – about 30 feet from him. He got on his feet and began to walk towards the light slowly. He was moving with caution and was feeling the floor before him, since he was unable to see it. He was able to determine the floor felt like a hard and raspy stone under his feet.

Mr. Y reached the light and he noticed it was the flame of a burning candle. This candle was attached to a holder, standing on a small, wooden antique table. There were no other items on the table. Thanks to the candle he was now able to see around him. He decided to take out his phone and call for help right away. He reached for his pocket and took out the phone – and he saw it was broken and perfectly dead! He couldn't understand what on earth had happened to it. He then checked the wristwatch: the date was correct, but the hands of the clock were stopped. He was baffled by all this.

Mr. Y took hold of the candle and lifted it up off the table. The light was illuminating the darkness and so he was trying to observe his surroundings more closely. It was then he noticed there was a white circle painted on the table – at the spot where the candle had been. A white line was drawn out of the circle; it went from the middle of the table to its edge, seeming to end there. But when he looked at it more closely, he noticed the line didn't end there; instead, it went on under the

table across its foot and all the way to the floor. Then
the line was painted on the floor, leaving the table and
disappearing into the dark. This line couldn't be found
by touch – only by using the light of the candle it could
be seen.

Mr. Y decided to follow the line; he was totally
clueless about the dark surroundings and thought the
line would lead him somewhere. He followed the line
through the darkness for about 15 minutes; usually it
went quite straight forward, but sometimes it curved,
swirled and even went zigzag. Finally he reached the
end of the line: it stopped to a large, wooden antique
door which was shut. He tried to open it, but it was of
no use. So he decided to knock the door and pound it
with his right hand a total of three times. Then – all of a
sudden – the door was opened and a bright light came
out of it. Since he had been in the dark until now, his
eyes got blinded by the light. He had to cover his eyes
and try to get them adjusted to the light. After a while
this goal was achieved. But what he then saw gave him
a big chill: there was an unknown man right in front of
him! This person was of the same size and the same
shape as he, wearing an old, worn-out hooded cape
used by monks. The hood was pulled over the man's
head, totally covering every inch of the face.

Mr. Y was feeling himself anxious; the stranger
didn't say a word and was just standing still. After
some time he was able to speak – asking the hooded
man where he was and what was going on. The
stranger, however, didn't answer to any of these
questions. But then he asked the man why had he ended
up here. After hearing this question the hooded figure
began to move all of a sudden, stepping aside from the
door and inviting him to enter it.   At first he was

unwilling to enter the door, since he knew nothing about the stranger's intentions. Finally, however, he gave up and went inside through the door – and it was closed behind him.

Now Mr. Y saw a long corridor before him – so long it seemed to be infinite. The walls of it were painted bright white and they were totally blank, with nothing on them. It was then the hooded man began to walk forward along this corridor. At first Mr. Y remained still, but soon he followed the man; he had to run to catch up and then he stopped just behind the man. So they kept on walking the corridor together – without saying a word to one other.

Finally – after a walk feeling like an eternity – they reached the end of the corridor. There a staircase was placed; it was made out of white stone and reaching up so high its top was nowhere to be seen – like it was going up to heaven itself! The two men began ascending these stairs, and they spoke nothing to each other. They went up for a long way – feeling like forever – along countless stairs. At last they reached the top; there was a door with golden decorations on it. This door was opened by itself and the men stepped inside – arriving to a great hall with bright white walls. But these weren't empty: there were numerous golden mirrors hanging on them – with silver plaques under each mirror. In the hall there was a single door and no windows. In addition to the mirrors and their plaques there were no other objects in this hall.

Mr. Y was puzzled by the strange place. But then the hooded man took hold of his shoulder, causing him to startle. The stranger, however, was calming him down by signing with his hands. Then he was led to the first mirror – at the left from the door. Its frame was made of gold and it was decorated with beautiful ornaments. Just then the hooded man was pointing towards this mirror. At first all he saw was his own reflection. But after a moment he was greatly distressed: the mirror image began to change! He rubbed his eyes in disbelief, but then he had to believe what he saw: his own image was being replaced with a different one! At first it was quite dim and unclear, but it slowly became clearer and more detailed. Finally it was perfectly clear: he saw a young woman sitting on a bed. She was holding a baby boy in her bosom. The baby cried, but she then waved her arms and sang a lullaby – and the cry was releaved. It seemed obvious the woman was the baby's mother. For some time he stood before the mirror and looked at this sight feeling confused. But then he saw the silver plaque under the mirror: it had a specific date engraved on it, with a day, a month and a year. When he had read this date, he was startled: it was the date of his own birth! He then looked at the mirror again. Right away he recognized the woman to be his own mother – sitting on a hospital bed in the room where he was born! So he was now looking at himself as a newborn child – and he was filled with feelings of anxiety and confusion: he had ended up in a place beyond comprehension – it was both fascinating and terrifying at the same time. Something odd was going to happen to him, or so he was expecting. However, he was unable to say anything to the man with the hood – so great was his amazement.

Then the stranger took Mr. Y by his shoulder and led him to the next mirror. Everything went just as before: now it was his christening. And in the next mirrors he saw the events following this: his first birthday, the beginning and the ending of his elementary school, his graduation from college and so on. He now understood he was being shown his whole life thus far. But why was he seeing it? At the moment he was unable to answer that.

Eventually Mr. Y had seen his entire previous life and had gone through all the mirrors – except the last one; it was different from all the others, because its frame wasn't gold but black onyx. He stepped before it and then begun to look at it – expecting to see another vision of his past. The mirror image began to change as it had before. But before the new image was clear, he saw the plaque under it. After reading the engraving he got a chill; it was the same date his wristwatch was displaying! He then looked back towards the mirror, since the image was fully visible now. The sight was horrifying: there was a car that had fallen off the road and become a wreck – with a man covered in blood on the driver's seat! When he looked at rhe image more closely, he was filled with fear and terror: the man in the mirror was he!

Mr. Y now realized it: he had been in a car-crash and he was dead now! That's why he had ended up in this intermediate state – this *limbo* – where he had seen his whole life from his birth to his death! He then realized what was the time his wristwatch was showing: it was the exact time of his death! So he tried to feel the pulse of his right wrist. It was just as he feared: no pulse at all!

It was then Mr. Y turned around and faced the man with the hood – still standing right behind him. He asked the stranger a question: are you my death? And the hooded figure answered by nodding its head. And then the stranger took hold of the hood and lowered it down. Now he saw the face under the hood – and he was struck with fear and terror! The figure looked exactly like him, but it didn't have human eyes: the holes for eyes were totally dark and black – looking like two pits going all the way down to the underworld!

Mr. Y realized what he was doing right now: he was face to face with his death, staring it right in the eyes! And then, suddenly, the dark man opened its mouth – just as dark as the eyes. A cloud of thick, black smoke began pouring out of it, surrounding Mr. Y all over. He didn't try to fight or escape it – he had accepted his death.

The Night Walkers

There are secrets which are meant to be revealed. But in addition to these there are secrets which should never be revealed. This is a story of what could happen when a forbidden secret is revealed. It is known as THE TALE OF THE NIGHT WALKERS.

It all began 800 years ago. Back then there was a glorious kingdom somewhere in Northern Europe. It was the place of peace and stability. It was ruled by a wise and gentle king, the people were happy and all was well. But this age of happiness didn't last forever. During one fateful night something horrible came about: the entire kingdom was plagued by a horde of terrible beasts – they slayed every human being they came across with! These creepy crawlers became known as THE NIGHT WALKERS! It was observed that these things were able to walk the earth only during nights; at dawn they all hid themselves since the sunlight was the most lethal venom to them.

These nocturnal beasts would get enraged and spread out all over the kingdom. They caused pain and suffering to everyone, so people lived in constant fear. Finally the king was able to get in touch with Zog the Ancient One, the most powerful shaman in the kingdom. Zog found out quite soon these things had come from the otherworld – a world that touches the human world. Somehow they had found a gateway between the two worlds and so were able to enter our world. Zog also found a way to send the monsters back to their side and to close their gateway for an indefinite time.

One night Zog went to the forest nearby the king's castle. He painted a magical seal on one specific rock.

Zog the Ancient One recited his spell and the gateway between the two worlds was opened. But this time it was working the opposite: it sucked all of these beasts back to where they came from and the seal shut the gateway behind them. The seal was covered with a huge pile of stones so nobody could ever find it and re-open the gate. For centuries the gate between the two worlds remained sealed. But finally came the time when this stability was disturbed.

One night there was a violent thunderstorm just above the rock with the magical seal. Suddenly, a bolt of lightning struck the rock and split it apart – and the seal as well! After this it has been told that THE NIGHT WALKERS are roaming the earth when the nights are dark. So if you hear strange noises in your house or get injured during nights like these, make sure to have some source of bright light near you. You can never know what lurks you in the darkness. It might even be one of THEM!

The Manic Memorandum

Bob had been locked up in an insane asylum for almost five years. During that time he didn't say a word or write anything. Bun then – all of a sudden – he began to write down things; some were weird, some hilarious, some disturbing, some boring. After Bob was done, he took his one last breath and dropped down dead. All that was left was his memorandum, and this is its content.

MY MEMORANDUM

I love my girlfriend!
However, she died yesterday after hitting the wall – literally! – with her car.
Luckily, I was the only one to witness this – excluding the gods and goddesses.
I picked up my girlfriend and brought her to my home.
She is now sitting before me in an armchair – totally still and quiet.
Her head is missing, and so is her left foot and also three fingers of her left hand.
But what does that matter?
I love my girlfriend!
I'm going to keep her always with me, and never let her be buried.
We'll stay together until death do us apart.
I make love to her every evening.
××××××××××××××××××××××××××××
Those who wish for death don't get it,
but those who don't wish for death get it.
Is bizzarre, isn't it!
××××××××××××××××××××××××××××

Corrosion for iron is the same as maggots for a carcass.
They disintegrate and return both to its basic elements.
×××××××××××××××××××××××××××

You are in a restaurant and you recieve a big, juicy
hamburger.
You can't prove nobody has spat between it.
Enjoy your meal!
×××××××××××××××××××××××××××

I was fishing at the deep ocean.
I caught a mermaid!
I lifted it to the boat, used a block to knock it out,
returned to the shore, took my knife, removed its head
and organs, cut and prepared it, cooked it in the oven
and ate it with a good appetite.
What? It was just a fish!
×××××××××××××××××××××××××××

A person with a closed circulation of food.
What it it?
It's a system where food returns to stomach in the form
of excrement by a plastic tube.
In the same way drink goes back to stomach as urine by
another tube.
But won't the person suffer constant troubles of
breathing and talking, not to mention the terrible taste?
No, because the tubes circulating excrement and urine
are surgically connected to the holes at right side of
stomach. In this way breathing, talking and taste won't
be affected. This is necessary since no human being
wants to take in exrement and urine in the same way as
normal food and drink.
Even so, humans find this closed circulation of food
very repulsive. But if was the way to solve the world
hunger, would that make it more pleasant?

If humans can get used to anything in the course of time, why not also to this closed circulation of food?

×××××××××××××××××××××××××××

It is said that people are ready to do anything for money. If they paid you 500 billion dollars in cash, would you rip out both of your eyeballs and eat them?

×××××××××××××××××××××××××××

Man has followed examples of nature in a plenty of ways. If he eats food, vomits it and eats the barf,
he is doing like cows and the other cattle do.
It is a perfectly natural thing.
So why are people disgusted of eating vomit?

×××××××××××××××××××××××××××

I drink 50 raw eggs every single day, for I'm smarter than a chicken!

×××××××××××××××××××××××××××

Wine is a drink for the wise,
anti-freeze is a drink for the fools.

×××××××××××××××××××××××××××

Infinite amount of pain, lasting infinite long.
It never decreases, it never increases.
If a person has always been in this state,
it is his normal state.
Even if he was told of a better state with less pain,
he is unable to comprehend it
and therefore unable to long for it.
This person only knows the infinite pain,
it is his pleasure.

×××××××××××××××××××××××××××

Is pain a part of being human or not?
Think about it!

×××××××××××××××××××××××××××

Once I attended a high school science class where I got sulfuric acid on my face.

Both of my eyes were melted by the acid.
Now – 20 years later – I remember the event and I'm very grateful it happened.
It was the only time I ever felt myself to be alive!
×××××××××××××××××××××××××××
I got two flies at a single strike.
Too bad they weren't women!
×××××××××××××××××××××××××××
What is the height of stupidity?
It is a person who thinks he's smart – but no-one else does!
×××××××××××××××××××××××××××
If a woman gets raped and becomes pregnant,
it has occurred to her in a natural way.
If a woman goes to a sperm bank and becomes pregnant by the sperm of a donor,
it has occurred to her in an unnatural way.
Therefore:
Getting raped as a way of getting pregnant is more moral than going to a sperm bank.
The sperm of a rapist is also fresh!
×××××××××××××××××××××××××××
Parents are telling a little boy how kids have footwear.
What he picures in his mind is a kid
with legs cut off from below the knees
and walking on these stumps.
These are footwear to him!
×××××××××××××××××××××××××××
It was hit by a brick.
It broke my skull and caused a bleeding in my brain.
Due to this I have lost my entire memory.
How blessed I am feeling now!
×××××××××××××××××××××××××××
Change is an inseperable part of life.

It happens at two levels – the spiritual and the physical. However, a dead person can no longer change except at the physical level when his body decays.

His soul will be the same for eternity – whether it is at the joy of heaven or at the furnace of hell.

×××××××××××××××××××××××××××

How many layers are in hell?
Go there for a visit and tell me!

×××××××××××××××××××××××××××

God created man as his own image,
Satan created himself as his own image.

×××××××××××××××××××××××××××

If God really existed, he could be discovered by using the sensory perception.
Those who think like this have the mind of an infant.

×××××××××××××××××××××××××××

The Worshiper of Fire

"For the Lord thy God is a consuming fire, even a jealous God."
(Deuteronomy 4:24)

INITIATION

I was standing alone in the middle of darkness.
There was no light in the room.
The floor was hard and moisty.
The room was located at the basement.
The door was locked with three big locks.
I knew there was no turning back.
They had already told me this clearly.
Now I had to face what was going to come.

I was staring into the darkness for hours.
It was silent everywhere, no sound could be heard.
Then, suddenly, my eyes saw something.
There was something glowing in the darkness.
It was like the glow of fiery coals.
They were glowing stronger and stronger.
At the same time light and heat increased in the room.
Finally the coals were fully ablaze.
In the rising flame I saw a divine figure.
He came to me and placed his hand upon my chest.

"And the angel of the Lord appeared unto him in a flame of fire out of the midst of a bush: and he looked, and, behold, the bush burned with fire, and the bush was not consumed." (Exodus 3:2)

*"Who maketh his angels spirits; his ministers a
flaming fire."* (Psalm 104:4)

*"And I looked, and, behold, a whirlwind came out of
the north, a great cloud, and a fire infolding itself, and
a brightness was about it, and out of the midst thereof
as the colour of amber, out of the midst of the fire."*
(Ezekiel 1:4)

*"His head and his hairs were white like wool, as whit
e
as snow; and his eyes were as a flame of fire;
And his
feet like unto fine brass, as if they burned in a
furnace;
and his voice as the sound of many waters."*
(Revelation 1:14–15)

PURGATORY

I was feeling burning pain upon my chest.
But this didn't surprise me at all.
For they had taught me this:
God is holy and pure, so his touch burns a sinner.
However, this touch purifies of sin eveyone who is able
to bear it.
It makes a person pure just like a furnace purifies gold
and silver.

So the burning pain wasn't a surprise to me.
But what came as a surprise was how insanely horrible
it actually was.
I have never felt a pain worse than it.
The divine figure's hand was burning my chest.

I was frozen still and I cried of pain.
I could feel my heart stopping and my entire body turning to dust.
And then the hand wasn't burning me anymore.

"Then said I, Woe is me! for I am undone; because I am a man of unclean lips, and I dwell in the midst of a people of unclean lips: for mine eyes have seen the King, the Lord of hosts. Then flew one of the seraphims unto me, having a live coal in his hand, which he had taken with the tongs from off the altar: And he laid it upon my mouth, and said, Lo, this hath touched thy lips; and thine iniquity is taken away, and thy sin purged." (Isaiah 6:5–7)

MYSTERY

I was able to breathe and fill my lungs with air.
I could feel my heart beating once more.
I opened my eyes and looked around.
The great flame was still burning before me.
But now he seemed to be calm.
I understood he had accepted me.
God had made me completely pure.

In an instant a number of torches was lighted up.
There were dozens of them, circling all around me and the great flame.
I was looking at these torches for a while.
Finally I was able to see each and every one of them had a person carrying it.
One of these torch-bearers stepped in the middle.
He also had an extra torch in his hand – the only one not yet burning.

He used the great flame to set it ablaze.
The torch was given to me and I took it in my hand.

*"And the three companies blew the trumpets, and
brake the pitchers, and held the lamps in their
left hands, and the trumpets in their right hands to
blow withal: and they cried, The sword of the
Lord, and of Gideon."* (Judges 7:20)

*"And it came to pass, as they still went on, and talked,
that, behold, there appeared a chariot of fire, and
horses of fire, and parted them both asunder; and
Elijah went up by a whirlwind into heaven."*
(2 Kings 2:11)

*"For every one shall be salted with fire, and every
sacrifice shall be salted with salt."*
(Mark 9:49)

*"And there appeared unto them cloven tongues like
as of fire, and it sat upon each of them."*
(Acts 2:3)

ILLUMINATION

They began to talk to me.
I heard words of kindness and gentleness.
I was warmly welcomed to the community of the pure
and sinless ones.
They all wore robes which were perfectly white.
I was given a robe just like these.
I took off my old clothes which were charred by fire.
I put on the white robe given to me.
Then I took the torch in my hand again.

They began to talk to me again.
I found out who they really were:
The messengers of God's fiery wrath.
They told me about the divine judgement that was about to fall upon the world very shortly.
Then I felt a fiery burning in my chest.
I knew I had to spread this message.

"And they shall go forth, and look upon the carcases of the men that have transgressed against me: for their worm shall not die, neither shall their fire be quenched; and they shall be an abhorring unto all flesh." (Isaiah 66:24)

"For since I spake, I cried out, I cried violence and spoil; because the word of the Lord was made a reproach unto me, and a derision, daily. Then I said, I will not make mention of him, nor speak any more in his name. But his word was in mine heart as a burning fire shut up in my bones, and I was weary with forbearing, and I could not stay." (Jeremiah 20:8–9)

"Is not my word like as a fire? saith the Lord; and like a hammer that breaketh the rock in pieces?" (Jeremiah 23:29)

"For, behold, the day cometh, that shall burn as an oven; and all the proud, yea, and all that do wickedly, shall be stubble: and the day that cometh shall burn them up, saith the Lord of hosts, that it shall leave them neither root nor branch." (Malachi 4:1)

"He shall baptize you with the Holy Ghost, and with fire. Whose fan is in his hand, and he will throughly purge his floor, and gather his wheat into the garner; but he will burn up the chaff with unquenchable fire." (Matthew 3:11–12)

"Then shall he say also unto them on the left hand, Depart from me, ye cursed, into everlasting fire, prepared for the devil and his angels." (Matthew 25:41)

"And now also the axe is laid unto the root of the trees:
every tree therefore which
bringeth not forth good fruit
is hewn down, and cast into the fire." (Luke 3:9)

"I am come to send fire on the earth; and what will I, if it be already kindled?" (Luke 12:49)

"And he cried and said, Father Abraham, have mercy on me, and send Lazarus, that he may dip the tip of his finger in water, and cool my tongue; for I am tormented in this flame." (Luke 16:24)

"And the smoke of their torment ascendeth
up for ever
and ever: and they have no rest day nor night, who worship the beast and his image, and whosoever receiveth the mark of his name." (Revelation 14:11)

"And whosoever was not found written in the book of life was cast into the lake of fire." (Revelation 20:15)

COMMUNION

A couple of weeks passed.
During this time I was one with them.
I became familiar with all torch-beareres.
At the same time I got to learn about myself.

We were the community of the divinely chosen ones.
We had been selected to be clean from sin and perfect
in every way.
The fire of God's fury had purified us from everything
wrong and false.
Quite soon I learned and accepted the idea that we were
better than everyone wlse.
The divine perfection had made us totally free from all
error and fallibility.
I found this idea very soothing and peace-giving.
I never again had to worry about if my words or deeds
were right or wrong.
I was part of a community which was always right.
This was declared by the divine justice.

The torch-bearers had no human to lead them.
All of us were brothers to each other.
The decisions which had to do with the community and
its members were always made at council meetings on
friday evenings.
It was when all torch-bearers got assembled together.
The meeting place was the same room at the basement
where the new members received the baptism of fire.
The council consisted of all the community members.
However, its purpose wasn't to make decisions.
Instead, the council was meant to receive the decisions
which the divine justice had declared.

Our holy duty was to execute them in real life.

The meeting began just like the initiation.
All council members were standing in the room which
was completely dark.
Everyone was holding his unlighted torch in his hand.
The torch-bearers stared into the darkness for a while.
Then the fiery glow began to appear in the dark.
It got stronger and the divine flame began to rise.
In an instant our torches were all ingnited by itself.
A voice like roaring thunder came out of the fire.
Our God began to speak and teach his will to us.

*"And when the Lord saw that he turned aside to
see, God called unto him out of the midst of the
bush, and said, Moses, Moses. And he said, Here am
I."*
(Exodus 3:4)

*"For I am the Lord your God: ye shall therefore
sanctify yourselves, and ye shall be holy; for I
am holy."*
(Leviticus 11:44)

*"And the Lord spake unto you out of the midst of the
fire: ye heard the voice of the words, but saw no
similitude; only ye heard a voice."*
(Deuteronomy 4:12)

*"I have said, Ye are gods; and all of you
are children of the most High."* (Ps. 82:6)

*"Ye know that the princes of the Gentiles exercise
dominion over them, and they that are great exercise*

authority upon them. But it
shall not be so among you:
but whosoever will be great among you, let him be
your minister." (Matt. 20:25–26)

PREDESTINATION

The torch-bearers had a firm belief that everything was predetermined by the divine providence.
The central idea was that humans have no free will and therefore no responsibility of their words or actions.
The divine providence made no mistakes and was unable to declare anything evil or wrong.
So there was no need to fear anything bad to happen.

We – the chosen ones – had been determined to speak and do only what was good and right.
Therefore I had no need to fear saying or doing anything evil or wrong.
Everything we spoke was right.
Everything we did was right.
I felt great freedom and peace.
Previously I had been very timid and insecure.
Now I was feeling myself brave and secure.

"According as he hath chosen us in him before the foundation of the world, that we should be holy and without blame before him in love." (Ephesians 1:4)

"But ye are a chosen generation, a
royal priesthood, an holy nation, a
peculiar people; that ye should shew forth the
praises of him who hath called you out
of darkness into his marvellous light." (1 Peter 2:9)

PREACHING

God had given us the gospel, the good news to preach.
It was the message of the divine fire about to burn the whole world to ash.
This God's judgement could only be avoided by joining the community of the torch-bearers.
I had already become part of this great gift of mercy.
I was compelled to tell it to others as well.

So I began to preach the gospel among my own relatives and my friends.
I wanted them to be saved with me.
Sadly I soon found out they weren't receiving my gospel.
They laughed, scorned and mocked my preaching.
At first I felt great sorrow for them.
Then it changed into burning anger towards them.
So I returned to my brothers in faith feeling down.

*"How beautiful upon the mountains are the feet of him
that bringeth good tidings, that publisheth peace; that
bringeth good tidings of good, that
publisheth salvation;
that saith unto Zion, Thy God reigneth!"* (Isaiah 52:7)

*"And I will shew wonders in the heavens and in the
earth, blood, and fire, and pillars of smoke. The
sun shall be turned into darkness, and the moon into
blood, before the great and the terrible day of the
Lord come. And it shall come to pass, that whosoever
shall call on the name of the Lord shall be delivered."*
(Joel 2:30–32)

"The time is fulfilled, and the kingdom of God is at hand: repent ye, and believe the gospel." (Mark 1:15)

"A prophet is not without honour, but in his own country, and among his own kin, and in his own house." (Mark 6:4)

"How then shall they call on him in whom they have not believed? and how shall they believe in him of whom they have not heard? and how shall they hear without a preacher? And how shall they preach, except they be sent?" (Romans 10:14–15)

OFFERING

At the next meeting I made all this known to my brothers.
I told them how my own relatives and friends had totally rejected my message of joy.
I was feeling great sorrow, pain and anger.
Then my brothers began to comfort me and told me not to blame myself for this.
They said the fault wasn't in me but in them who had not believed my preaching.
The gospel had no effect on them since their souls were impure and corrupted.

In addition, the brothers let me know there was one way how my relatives and friends could still be saved.
In fact, they were already working on it.
I was overjoyed when I heard about this.
But then I found out what they were going to do:

The impure and corrupted souls could only be saved by
purification through divine fire, that is, by burning their
living bodies of flesh as an offering!

*"And if thine eye offend thee, pluck it out, and cast it
from thee: it is better for thee to enter into life with
one eye, rather than having two eyes to be
cast into hell
fire."* (Matthew 18:9)

*"If any man's work abide which he hath built
thereupon, he shall receive a reward. If any
man's work
shall be burned, he shall suffer loss: but he
himself shall be saved; yet so as by fire."* (1
Corinthians 3:14–15)

*"But if our gospel be hid, it is hid to them that
are lost."*
(2 Corintians 4:3)

PRAYING

I was unable to get any sleep during the following
night.
Great pain and distress had overtaken me.
In a couple of days I was supposed to go with the others
to perform this murder by fire.
Just the tought of this caused my heart to hurt.
I couldn't do it, I knew it was wrong.

For hours I was writhing on my bed and weeping as
well.
I was disturbed and totally unable to think.

I didn't know what to do and felt myself to be lost.

In the silence of the night I began to pray in the way my mother had taught me as a child.
It was a very beautiful and tender prayer, filled with the peace, mercy and love of God.
When I finished praying, there was a peaceful and safe feeling in my heart.
Then I knew I had found the right path.
I understood what I had to do.

"But thou, when thou prayest, enter into thy closet, and when thou hast shut thy door, pray to thy Father which is in secret; and thy Father which seeth in secret shall reward thee openly." (Matthew 6:6)

"The effectual fervent prayer of a righteous man availeth much." (Jacob 5:16)

ABSOLUTION

In the same night I made my silent escape.
The first thing in the morning was I went to the nearest police station without any hesitation.
When I stepped inside, I told them everything right away.
I provided the police with every piece of info I knew of the torch-bearers and their community.
I also revealed the secret location of their hideout.
The cult had to be stopped and wiped away forever.

It has been seven years since all this happened.

I'm still in pain and sorrow when I remember how they burned themselves to death when the police found them.

Now I can see how evil and wrong that community was.

It didn't worship God but his wrath.

Finally God gave his judgement by destroying it.

I was the only one to get out of there alive.

Even though I had seen great miracles there, they weren't godly but demonic.

It was a great miracle I was saved from this cult.

God wants me to go on with my life, I believe so.

"The sun was risen upon the earth when Lot entered into Zoar. Then the Lord rained upon Sodom and upon Gomorrah brimstone and fire from the Lord out of heaven." (Genesis 19:23–24)

"Thou shalt not bow down thyself to them, nor serve them: for I the Lord thy God am a jealous God, visiting the iniquity of the fathers upon the children unto the third and fourth generation of them that hate me; And shewing mercy unto thousands of them that love me, and keep my commandments." (Exodus 20:5–6)

"Fear not: for I have redeemed thee, I have called thee by thy name; thou art mine." (Isaiah 43:1)

"For every tree is known by his own fruit." (Luke 6:44)

"For God so loved the world, that he gave his only begotten Son, that whosoever believeth in him should

not perish, but have everlasting life." (John 3:16)

"And no marvel; for Satan himself is transformed into an angel of light. Therefore it is no great thing if his ministers also be transformed as the ministers of righteousness; whose end shall be according to their works." (2 Corinthians 11:14–15)

The Star Demon

"It was just
a colour out of space –
a frightful messenger from unformed realms
of infinity..."

H. P. Lovecraft

1. Hot Summer

It was a beautiful, sunny day of spring. Snow was gone, the birds had returned and summer was about to begin. There were just a few days left until the semester ended and the summer break fully started. Lisa (age 18) and her boyfriend David (age 20) were already getting prepared for their upcoming trip. They were going to spend the whole June at a farm belonging to Lisa's family. Her dad Chris (age 48) and mom Anne (age 44) were excited to spend the whole month at country with the kids, far away from their busy urban environment. The whole group was preparing carefully so everything would be ready for the graduation day. They were going to begin their trip on that very day. Lisa's grandparents Billy (age 75) and Karen (age 70) were also living near the farm. They were already expecting their daughter Anne and her family for a summer visit.

Lisa woke up at her student apartment. She was lying next to sleeping David on her bed, after a wild night. She put on her glasses and looked around her. They were both naked and also quite exhausted. Then Lisa could feel something sticky against her right thigh, so she lifted up the blanket. She saw her boyfriend lying on his left side and resting his cock – about 6 inches long – on her right thigh. The condom had slipped off and it had spilled its content all over her thigh and the bed. Lisa got up, put on her bra and panties, picked up the condom and put it in the trash can. She then took paper towels and cleaned the mess as well as she could – while David was sleeping. After this she went to the bathroom and began to shower herself. She spent about ten minutes in the bathroom.

When Lisa had finished cleaning up herself and opened the door, she saw David had woken up. He was lying on the bed and looking at his girlfriend wearing a bathrobe. He was still totally naked and his cock began to grow hard again. Lisa knew his boyfriend was ready to make love to her again. In an instant she didn't feel to be tired anymore; so she took off her robe, uncovering her fine curves and bouncing boobs. Lisa was a science nerd and also quite kinky in bed. David was used to this since women with high intelligence are able to think a lot more creative ways to have sex than normal people. Lisa took her vibrator, lubricated it and turned it on. She then took a lemon-flavored condom, put it in her mouth and placed it on her boyfriends hard cock by using her mouth. Lisa got upon David, placing her pussy just above his cock. Then she took the turned-on vibrator and inserted in her butthole all the way. After this, she put her lover's cock in her pussy and slid it inside all the way. Lisa was now very hot and so was David. So the couple had kinky sex for breakfast; he grabbed her bouncing boobs while she rubbed her pussy for extra pleasure. This act culminated in a huge orgasm – on both sides: David's cock filled the condom so it was about to burst, and Lisa got a massive squirt out of her pussy. She then sat on her lover for some time until his cock was all floppy. Lisa kissed David and felt so pleased to have him as her lover; she thought her pussy could only be satisfied by his amazing 6 inch cock, since no-one else could give her orgasms. In fact, it was David who had given Lisa her very first orgasm and she had determined they were meant to each other. She never stopped thanking God for David in her daily prayers.

Lisa and David both took a shower, got dressed and had some breakfast together. Then she started to pack the most important items to take with her to the summer trip. She ended up taking her favorite book (*Murder on the Orient Express* by Agatha Christie), her teddybears (Winnie and Minnie) and – as the most important – her telescope and notebook. Ever since childhood Lisa had been interested in the starry sky; its beauty, vastness and wonderfulness impressed her every time she lifted her eyes towards the sky with stars. Lisa had worked hard to be able to buy herself a professional telescope. A couple of months ago she finally had succeeded. Lisa was glad to test the telescope at the balcony of her apartment house. Thus far she had seen the zodiac, a few planets and some shooting stars. She had written all her observations into her notebook with the name of the phenomenon, location and date. However, the night lights of the city covered up most of the stars. Therefore she had decided to take all of her equipment with her to the country; for the stars would surely be seen better there than at the city. Lisa was quite excited about the upcoming trip to the country.

David was standing at her door and knocked it.

"*Yeah, what is it?*", said Lisa and turned around to face the door. Then her boyfriend opened it.

"Listen up, babe! I just thought of something.", David said to her.

"Really? What is it, Dave?", asked Lisa.

"It's about your place, that farm.", he went on. *"What kind of opportunities for sanitation or bathing is there?"*

"So you mean if our farm has a bathroom or a toilet?", said Lisa.

"Right!", replied David.

"Well, yes and no!", Lisa told him. *"It has an outhouse and a wood-heated sauna. It doesn't have a running water, so we have to get it from the well."*

"You're kidding me, Liz!", David grunted.

"It belongs to my grandparents, a couple of old farmers. So what did you expect?", Lisa was wondering.

"Nothing luxurious, but also nothing shaggy.", David told her. *"So how am I going to wash my hair and get it in shape if I can't see it in the mirror?"*

Lisa began to laugh at his vanity.

"That's not a problem!", she answered. *"All it takes from you is to stop shaping your hair with wax. Just wash and comb it, that's all."*

"You mean I have to keep my hair unwaxed and unshaped for almost a month?", David asked with a scared expression upon his face. *"And what about the fact there is no shower?"*

"Maybe not, but it doesn't matter. The sauna is going to make up for it quite nicely.", said Lisa.

"Oh yeah, and how's that?", asked David.

"It is the kind of sauna where we go totally naked. And when it gets hot and steamy, my pussy will be so hot and wet you can't even imagine!", she said and tried to seduce him.

David got very excited about her words. It got to him so strong the front of his shorts began to bulge. Lisa was unable to believe her eyes; how was it possible his cock had already regained its strength? But he then decided to tell her. He showed her a tiny blue bottle.

"What's in that bottle?", she asked.

"Don't you know it?", he replied.

Lisa took a closer look at the bottle. She then knew what it was; her failed attempt in creating a hair growth formula for the science fair this spring!

"I took it just by accident last week.", David explained to her. *"Turned out it does grow, not hair but your sexual desire. Just try it!"*

So David gave the bottle to Lisa. She took a sip of the blue liquid it contained. Its effect was surprising: she could feel her pussy tingling and burning with desire! Lisa was unable to control herself: she ran to David and tossed him on the bed. She quickly took off her skirt and panties – uncovering her wet and dripping pussy. She then pulled down his shorts and his hard cock sprang up. Lisa was so excited she pulled a real stunt: she jumped in the air and landed her pussy right upon his cock. It went inside her rapidly and her butt slammed upon her lover's hips. The result was explosive: David was cumming right away, filling her pussy with a load so huge it was gushing out of her pussy. Then Lisa was also cumming and gave out a huge squirt; it gave her such a powerful boost she got launched in the air like a rocket – and she landed on the bed next to him! Lisa looked at the hot cum flowing out of her pussy. But she then realized they had used no protection, so she could have become pregnant. This was not something Lisa had wanted – or neither David – and so she began to weep.

He embraced her and tried to comfort her. But she refused to be calm and just kept crying. After a while Lisa got herself pulled together. She was looking at her boyfriend and was sniffing her nose. David looked back.

"What are we going to do, baby?", said Lisa.

"What do you mean, Liz?", asked David.

"If you got me pregnant, we can't have a child. Right?", replied Lisa in despair.

"Yeah, you know it, sexy!", David smiled at her. She slapped him on his left cheek with force.

"Ouch! What the fuck! That really hurt!"

"Asshole! There's nothing to smile about!"

"Yes, there is, Liz! You can't be pregnant, there is no fucking way!"

"Huh? How can you know?"

"Take this cum and look at it in the microscope."

Lisa took a sample and put in upon a glass plate. She placed it under her trusty microscope and looked at it. The sample didn't have any sperm in it; it had no seed!

"Just temporary. Your formula did it. Nice, huh?"

"Yeah, very nice!", said Lisa with a sigh of relief.

2. Day of Graduation

It was Saturday when Lisa and David graduated from their college. All of their parents were present at the ceremony – taking pictures and feeling proud of them. Both of them had finished years of studies and working.

In addition they were given special rewards from their college: Lisa was given an honorary Ph.D degree for her achievements in the field of science, and David got his name in the Hall of Fame of the college football team. They and their parents were just as positive as the weather outside: the birds were singing and the sun was shining without a cloud in the sky. Everything was just perfect for the first day of the summer break.

After returning home they changed their formal clothes for the normal. Then they began the road trip to the countryside. The car belonging to Lisa's parents had been packed at the previous evening, so they were able to start their journey right after graduation. However, they went through all the stuff one last time to see if anything was missing; this was smart since many necessary things were not there and had to be supplied. Lisa was checking with care the telescope since it was the most important of her items; it had to remain stable and secure so it would not be broken. Each of them was checking through his or hers own stuff for quite a while. Finally the white car was able to leave Lisa's home and to start the road trip.

During the first half of the trip they didn't talk much to one other; Lisa's parents were listening to the car radio while Lisa and David were online with their phones – holding hands as they did so. However, something very embarrassing happened when the second half of the trip began. Lisa was checking the latest astronomical news and found out about a great meteor shower coming on the next Wednesday. She was overjoyed and turned to show it to David. But then she saw his phone and was shocked.

David was watching porn on his smart phone! Lisa was angry for she was feeling jealous for this. But at the same time she was afraid her parents might find out about all the kinky stuff she and her boyfriend had done. She was quite sure they wouldn't like it, since they had always been quite conservative in their values; sex was to be practiced only by a married couple – masturbation, pornography and pre-marital sex were all out of question! If they found out about her and her boyfriend screwing around her apartment, they might force them to break up!

Lisa knew she had to move fast. So she began to speak with her parents about a very specific subject:

"It was such a horrible thing!", she told them.

"What are you talking about?", Chris asked.

"I just saw a commercial of a porn site!", she said to both of her parents.

"Those are so disgusting! Everyone who looks after porn is a pervert!", Anne gave her a fast reply.

"I know, right! It has to stop!", Lisa answered.

When David heard this, he realized what he was doing and in what company. Luckily, he was able to stay cool and close all the porn before Chris and Anne saw it. He then sent Lisa some text messages and she replied:

"Thanks, babe! You saved my ass!"

"No problem, my stud! Be more careful!"

"Sure! I'll give you my special gift in bed!"

"That's sweet! But you'll have to wait until it's safe for you to give it to me."

"Okay, I cum back to you! Bye!"

"Yes, I'm cuming too! Tschüss!"

After driving for a couple of hours the travelling company arrived to their destination. The farm seemed just like Lisa had always remembered it; she felt like time had come to a complete stop around here. The car went all the way to the front of the house and was then stopped. The doors opened and they began to unload the luggage. Lisa's grandparents Billy and Karen came to meet them.

3. The Mysterious Star

The first days of their summer vacation went quite fast. On Sunday it was a day of rest; Lisa and David spent the whole day relaxing around the farm. However, she didn't have sex with him since it was the day of going to church. On Monday it was a sunny day; so the young couple went to the nearby lake for a swim and to have a picnic. But Lisa and David didn't make love since they had forgotten to bring along any protection. On Tuesday it was a day of helping; they spent the whole day doing all sorts of tasks around the farm – and afterwards were too tired to screw each other. When it was Wednesday, Lisa got very excited about the following evening; she would be able to watch the great meteor shower by her telescope! David wanted to make love to her, but Lisa refused him; all her thoughts were already focused on the upcoming evening – when the stars would show up. David got angry because of her.

Finally the day was going towards evening and it was beginning to get dark. When the grandfather clock struck the time 10 p.m., Lisa went outside on the balcony to observe the stars with her dad Chris and her mom's dad Billy; her mom Anne and her mom's mom Karen were so worn out of the daily tasks they had already gone to sleep. Lisa and the others ascended the stairs to the second floor. Then Billy took a special key and used it to open the door to the balcony. Lisa stepped outside and saw the clear sky full of stars opening above the balcony; it was perfect for observing the stars. When all three of them were standing on the balcony, Lisa took out her telescope and started to put it in order; she placed it firmly standing upon a tripod, took out the lens covers and aimed the telescope towards the stars. Lisa placed her left eye upon the lens piece and started to adjust the focus of the system. At that moment David went upstairs and to the balcony. He was upset for Lisa who had refused to satisfy his desire towards her.

"Can you see anything?", Chris asked her.

"Not yet!", said Lisa.

"Let me take a look!", David provoked her.

"First it must be set right, you fool!", she grunted.

"Hey, watch your language!", Chris told her.

"Miss Lisa, you apologise David this instant!", said Billy with a harsh tone.

"Okay, I'm sorry, Dave!", she sighed and felt herself to be frustrated.

This apology was far from sincere, but it was enough for David and the other two. But at the very moment Lisa gasped for joy and got very thrilled.

"Hey, I see something now!", reported Laura.

"What do you see?", her dad questioned.

"I see a star, another one and third one. And even more. Hang on! Yes! Right! There is the good old constellation, that great dipper!", Lisa announced.

"It can be seen with bare eyes.", said David with a lot of scorn.

Lisa turned the telescope for a bit and she looked again through the lens.

"Now I can see Sirius!", she yelled and turned it.

"*And there are the Pleiades!*", said Lisa with a lot of excitement.

Then she finally saw it – the spectacle she had waited with such a deep desire.

"*I saw a meteor! Another one! Third one!*", she let out her thrilled joy.

So began the longed-for meteor shower and the sky was filled with tiny flashes of light.

"*Let me see now!*", David commanded her.

Finally Lisa gave room for her boyfriend and so he got to look through the lens. She took out her notebook and began to write down with enthusiasm the phenomena she had seen. The sky was clear and filld with stars – and no lights of the city were interfering with the observation. Lisa was very pleased; her telescope was fully functional.

David, however, was still holding grudge for her. He had been in this celibacy against his will for over four days. He was feeling burning lust for Lisa, but she didn't let him satisfy it. So David began cursing Lisa in his mind and thinking evil thoughts; he wanted to fuck her, rape her, beat her, crush her – and then start all over again! He even promised to become the devil's slave if he was given the power to do all this to Lisa. And he promised it now!

In an instant – out of nowhere – something weird appeared to David through the telescope.

"*Hey! A new star just began shining in the sky!*" he cried aloud to everyone else.

Lisa was struck by awe when she heard this. She had checked all the information about the sky tonight, but besides the meteor shower there was nothing else. Lisa then stopped doing her notes, got herself up and looked towards the sky. Now she saw it herself: there really was a new, bright star up in the sky! Its light was so powerful it was perfectly visibe to everyone. Upon seeing this Lisa started to wonder what could it be. The only astronomical explanation she was able to think of was a supernova. She was familiar with massive stars whose life-cycle ended with a great explosion – visible even to the earth. But then she thought why she hadn't found any news about this. Apparently it must be a supernova that no astronomer had been able to predict. Yes, that must be it! This idea gave Lisa's mind some cool-down so she was able to admire this mysterious star.

For quite a while they were all looking at the star, like they were under a spell. David was still looking at it with his left eye through the telescope lens. The star was wonderfully beautiful due to its size, its brightness – and its color! At first it was violet, then indigo, then light blue, then green, then yellow, then orange, then red – and then violet again! The color was changing all the time, going through the whole spectrum of the visible light – all the colors of a rainbow! Lisa had never seen a star like that –or even heard or read about such a thing. So she thought this might be a new and remarkabe scientific discovery – maybe even worth a Nobel price! Inspired by this thought, she again took her notebook and began to write down as much as she could about the star.

Up to this moment the wonderful star had been totally still in the night sky – without any movement to any direction. Then, suddenly, David said something that startled all the others:

"Look! Now it began to vibrate!"

So Lisa, her father and grandpa looked at the star more closely. And it really was vibrating! Its movement reminded them of the last winter and how cold it had been; it seemed like the star was shivering! At first the vibrating was quite peaceful, but it was gradually increasing itself. Finally the star was vibrating so greatly it almost seemed like there was two stars instead of one! And then – all of a sudden – it happened: the star fired a beam of light – like a flash of lightning – and it struck the telescope lens! This resulted in a huge, blinding blast, forcing everyone to cover their eyes and cry out in pain. For a long while all they could see were flashing spots and swirls in their eyes, for they were blinded by the flash. When it finally was ended, Lisa, Chris and Billy opened their eyes. They saw each other and were relieved, since their eyes hadn't lost their sight. This relief, however, was going to be much shorter than they thought. Now their eyes looked at something that gave them chills of fear: David was lying on the floor before the telescope – and completely lifeless! Chris rushed to him and tried his pulse; his heartbeat was there and he was breathing – this was the good news. But the bad news came shortly, when they tried to wake him up: he remained totally unconcious – it was impossible to wake him up!

Billy and Chris took hold of the arms and legs. They picked David up and carried him inside the house. He was then laid on a soft rug, upon his right side. Lisa was staying by her lover's side to make sure his condition was stable. Meanwhile, her father Chris was calling the emergency number and ordering an ambulance. Grandpa Billy went to wake up her mother and grandmother since they were unaware of David's condition. Lisa stepped out to the balcony and she looked up towards the night sky: the mysterious star had disappeared!

4. The Dark Eye

It took about half an hour before the ambulance arrived to the yard. It stopped in front of the main building and its back doors were opened. A pair of white-clothed men rushed out of the car, took a stretcher out of the back and began to carry them towards the house. The front door was already open, with Chris and Billy standing on the porch. The men got in without hesitation. They were led to the room where Anne and Karen were sitting next to David – who was still totally unconcious. The emergency men performed the usual procedures: they checked David's pulse, blood pressure and other vitals – and they all turned out fine. Then the men lifted him onto the stretcher, fastened the safety belts and resumed their positions to carry it – the other men at David's head and the other at his feet. Lisa was also standing beside them.

Then something unexpected came to be: both of David's eyes got fully opened! This startled everybody around him and they all took a few steps away. After that they stepped back to him and looked at his opened eyes. The sight was disturbing: David's left eye – the one he had used to observe the star through the lens – was now completely black! David was blue-eyed, but there was none of the old color left – or even any white around it; this looked like the pupil had grown over its boundaries and had swallowed up all other parts of the left eye! This sight shocked everyone standing around him. Although David's right eye was fine, this gave no reason for them to calm down. Everybody remained still for some time, looking at David with a deep silence – as if they were all attending his funeral service.

Finally it was Lisa who dared to approach him; she stepped right next to her boyfriend and she reached her face above his. David was still without any kind of movement or sound – while both of his eyes were staring towards the room ceiling. Lisa was then focusing her eyes upon David's left eye – the dark one. For a while she was looking intently at it to see some sign of living. But this waiting seemed to be useless, since he didn't even blink his eyes. But then – all of a sudden – Lisa cried out and fell backwards on the floor! While she was looking into the dark eye, she had felt a struck of terror: it had seemed to her like there was a dark, shadowy figure in his eye, looking right back at her! Now Lisa was sitting on the floor next him – shivering and panting with fear. Anne came to her daughter, knelt down and embraced her.

The emergency men were very baffled; they had never seen anything like this. They tried to wake David up, but he still didn't respond. So they lifted him up and carried him all the way to the ambulance. Lisa's parents and grandparents were then discussing with the men and telling they were going to visit David tomorrow. Finally the men got in and began their journey to the hospital.

Lisa was standing at the bottom of the staircase, opposite the front door. Her family stepped inside it, with her mom as the last one. She closed the door behind her.

Everyone was upset and sad for what happened to David, but especially Lisa's mom; Anne was very fond of David and he was like a dear son to her. She sobbed.

"*Let's get some sleep!*", said Anne and sniffed.
"*Mom, there was a thing in his eye!*", told Lisa.

"What kind of thing?"
"I don't know, it looked like a shadow!"
"Well, just your own reflection, that's all!"

Lisa didn't believe this; she had felt the presence of evil!

5. The Light of the Body

Three days passed. David was still at the hospital and his condition was the same as before; he was lying on his bed without any movement and his eyes were constantly open. Lisa and her parents had visited David every day and they had asked the doctors about his condition. Sadly, they had always received the same answer: it was still unknown. The doctors had never seen anything like this; David's breathing and all his vital functions were totally normal, but his conciousness was dark. Their brain scanner was unable to detect any signs of thoughts, sensory perception or any other activity. However, he wasn't braindead and all his neurons were perfectly fine. David's head was like a light bulb with no power turned on. He was confined in his own patient room at the hospital. There he was given nutrional solution into his bloodstream and from time to time drops of moisture in his eyes. David's dark eye was still a total mystery and uncomparable to any previous cases. Lisa and her family were worried about David, but they hoped for the best – and kept waiting for news of his recovery.

Lisa had found life at the countryside to be quite soothing; the sunny days, the flower-covered meadows and the farmyard animals were helping her to think much less about David and his dark eye; while the happy things were on the top of her mind, there was no room for the sad things. Life went on like this for a few days.

Then another odd event happened to Lisa at the living room; she was sitting at the floor and was working on a jigsaw puzzle – of 500 pieces and its theme was the universe, filled with stars, planets and galaxies. Lisa had just put the final piece in its place and was admiring the result. Then, suddenly, she heard a banging sound. Lisa got frightened and jumped up on her feet. She then began to look around the living room – and she noticed a book had fallen out of the cabinet and then landed on the floor. Lisa went closer and saw the book was wide open. She then noticed what book it was: an old Bible – King James Version – belonging to her grandparents. Lisa looked at the text more closely and one specific passage drew her attention. It was part of Jesus' Sermon on the Mount and read like this:

*"The light of the body is the
eye: if therefore thine eye
be single, thy whole body shall be full of light.
But if thine eye be evil, thy whole body shall be full
of darkness. If therefore the light that is in thee
be darkness, how great is that darkness!"*
Matthew 6:22–23

These words of Jesus gave chills to Lisa; she recalled all too well the dark eye and the evil shadow she had seen in it. Could this be the kind of darkness Jesus was talking about? Was David's body unable to move since it was full of darkness? Lisa found questions like these frightening, but she was unable to pass them over. It was not possible for her to be careless at the country any longer, because David might be in a great danger.

Lisa's conscience was calling her to go and help him before it was too late. She decided to follow the call.

6. The Dark Abyss

Lisa was standing at the main entrance of the hospital with her dad and mom at 11.05 a.m. About five minutes later they reached the patient room where David was at the moment. He was lying on the bed and staring at the ceiling with eyes wide open. There was a droplet-bottle attached to his left elbow and a pulse-measuring sensor at the left-hand index finger. At the very moment the nurse used the moisturing drops upon David's eyes. Then she greeted his girlfriend and her parents – and left the room to inform the doctor about their arrival.

Lisa took one of the small chairs in the room and moved it to the right side of her lover's bed. She sat down on the chair and took hold of David's right hand. It felt very different than before and it was like the hand of a stranger. If Lisa wasn't aware it was David's hand, she wouldn't have known who the person in the bed was. Her eyes got wet and streams of tears began to flow upon her cheeks. Chris and Anne were standing at the left side of the bed. They were deeply troubled for both of the kids.

The doctor entered the room at 11.30 a.m. He greeted everyone and then began to speak with them. Last night there had turned up something very intriguing in the research and he wanted to show it. The doctor invited all of them to come with him to the X-ray department and to have a look at the new X-ray photos taken yesterday. Dad and mom went with him, but Lisa didn't want to; she was afraid to see what – or who – could be detected in those images. The others left the room and closed the door.

For a few minutes there was peace and quiet in the room. The only sound was the soothing "beep, beep" of the pulse measuring. Lisa's tears had stopped and she felt herself to be tired. Then – while being half asleep and with her eyes closed – she began to remember the text she had read yesterday. Lisa was reciting the words in a slow, whispering sound: "*The ... light ... of ... the ... body ... is ... the ... eye: ... if ... therefore ... thine ... eye*
... be ... single, ... thy ... whole ... body ... shall ... be ... full ... of ... light. ... But ... if ... thine ... eye ... be ... evil, ... thy ... whole ... body ... shall ... be ... full ... of ... darkness. ... If ... therefore ... the ... light ... that ... is ... in ... thee ...
be ... darkness, ... how ... great .. is ... that ... darkness!"

Lisa had barely said the last word, when it came to pass: in an instant – all of a sudden – David got up to sit on the bed and grabbed her hair with both of his hands! She cried and tried to break loose, but it was useless; his grip was so strong she could imagine herself wrestling a bear! David lifted Lisa up from the chair and pushed her face against his own. Lisa opened her eyes and got scared by what she saw: David's left eye – the dark one – seemed to her like a window that revealed what was inside him – and it was a deep, infinite darkness! Now Lisa saw a bottomless pit opening before her eyes, leading to a world unknown and without light. At the same time it was both frightening and fascinating to her. Lisa felt like she was being called and pulled towards that abyss of darkness. She then saw something horrible; countless black arms

– more like tentacles – came out of darkness! They grabbed hold of her and began to pull her to the pit! She struggled and tried to get free, but they were too powerful: Lisa fell down and into the pit – into the infinite darkness!

Some time passed. Then Lisa's parents and the doctor came back to the room. As they entered all seemed to be just as before: David was still lying on the bed and was staring at the ceiling. But then they noticed there was something in his hands. When Chris and Lisa came closer and looked at his hands, they were startled; David was holding a bunch of Lisa's hair in his hands! They started to panic and search for her, but they found nothing: Lisa had disappeared with no trace!

7. The Face of Evil

Lisa woke up and opened her eyes. She saw darkness around her; it was so thick it was almost tangible. It was at first just strange and confusing to her. Lisa couldn't comprehend where she was and how she'd gotten there. She remembered falling down the dark pit, but wasn't able to determine if it had been real or not. To be sure Lisa pinched her right arm and felt pain: she was awake and not dreaming! This gave her even more anxiety and fear; apparently she was now in the middle of the same darkness she had seen in David's left eye. But Lisa had no idea what kind of place this was; it was dark all over and no details could be seen in the surroundings. There was also perfect silence everywhere – reminding her of the shadow of death!

For a while Lisa kept walking straight forward and fumbling in the dark. But then she saw an odd thing: a tiny bright light suddenly appeared close to her.

It was like a star – the kind she had seen multiple times in the sky. While she was observing it she noticed there were even more stars appearing around her: they were coming one by one in an increasing pace! Soon the stars were so many Lisa was unable to count them. It seemed she was standing in the middle of the universe – with all the stars gathered around her!

Lisa was deeply amazed by this sight and she was wondering it greatly: the stars were hovering all over and around her – just like fireflies in the dark. They were glowing white and expelling the darkness around them. This went on for a while – and then Lisa saw yet another weird sight: one of the stars began to lose its light and to grow darker. Its light faded and faded – and finally it was perfectly gone. Only a dark star with no light was left; it could only be observed against the other stars which still had their light. Lisa recalled she had read about stars who begin to lose light when their hydrogen is getting low. She had also read about the red giants, the white dwarfs and the black holes the dying star could turn into. But none of these was like the dark star Lisa was now seeing before her eyes. So she began to think it was no ordinary star.

After Lisa had been watching this dark star for some time she noticed it began to change its spherical form: first it became a formless cloud of gas which then began to gradually get a new form. She was observing this metamorphosis with amazement and soon there was something very unexpected: out of this dark cloud began to appear things that looked like bodyparts: head, arms, legs – and also wings and tail! Suddenly Lisa was struck with a great terror for she knew the figure standing before her: it was the shadow thing she had seen in David's dark eye! She then realized what this place was: she was inside David – literally! To Lisa this apperared very insane; he had been inside her many times, but now she was inside him! She was in the middle of the very darkness that had filled his boyfriend's body. That has to be the answer!

Lisa was so frightened she was unable to move. In the meanwhile the cloud of gas was gaining an even more distinguished and recognizable form: it had great wings just like a bat and the tail and tongue like a lizard. There were sharp claws – like those of a bear – on its hands and feet. Its body was pitch-black and as dark as a black hole. There was a pair of horns upon its head – just like those of an ox. Its mouth was filled with razor-sharp teeth and its eyes were burning red. There was no more room for Lisa to be mistaken: it was a demon!

8. The Battle of Light and Darkness

Lisa was standing still and shaking while looking at the beast in front of her. Its beginning had been in a tiny star just the size of a marble. However, out of this cosmic egg was born this giant – almost 15 feet high – demon! It was looking at her with its sinister eyes; these were like two burning coals in its pitch-black head. The monster gave her a mean grin and revealed its horrible teeth; they were as thin and sharp as sowing needles – and their number was in thousands! Between these teeth a long red tongue was slithering out, waving itself up and down. This whole time the demon was standing still and being totally quiet – just like a predator lurking for its prey. For a long time Lisa was so terrified she was unable to talk or move. She had learned at school you should't make any loud sounds or sudden moves before a beast. But Lisa was now being still and quiet because of fear and terror – the kind she had never faced in her life!

Finally Lisa was able to open her mouth and she said to the demon with a shivering voice:

"Wh-wh-who a-are yo-yo-you?"

When the demon heard this it burst into a creepy and unrestrained laughter. Its voice was an ear-shattering screech – just like every crow and raven of the world was crowing at the same time! After laughing for a while it began to talk with a piercing voice, just like a thunderbolt! In the middle of this terrible noise Lisa was able to hear the demonic words:

"I-AM-THE-LORD-OF-CHAOS-!", the chilling response echoed.

The horrfied Lisa then pulled herself together and asked her second question:

"Wh-what do yo-you want?", stuttered Lisa.

"TO-RETURN-ALL-THINGS-BACK-TO-THE-STATE-THEY-WERE-BEFORE-THE-ONE-WHOSE-NAME-I-CANNOT-SAY-CREATED-ORDER-OUT-OF-CHAOS-!", the demon rumbled.

"W-wh-why are you inside David?", she asked.

"THE-ONE-WHOSE-NAME-I-CANNOT-SAY-CREATED-MAN-TO-BE-HIS-OWN-IMAGE-AND-PUT-THE-COSMOS-INSIDE-HIM-WHEN-I-DESTROY-THE-INSIDE-OF-ONE-MAN-THE-COSMOS-INSIDE-HIM-WILL-BECOME-CHAOS-!", said the demon.

"I have the living God at my side!", shouted Lisa triumphantly and began to pray for help. She did this in a way she was taught at Sunday school and was asking God as honestly as she could. But nothing

happened: the only answer Lisa got to her prayer was silence.

The demon saw all of this and began to laugh once more; this time there clearly was more mockery and scorn in its voice. Then it began to beat her with words:

"YOU-FOOL-YOU-THINK-THE-ONE-WHOSE-NAME-I-CANNOT-SAY-IS-GOING-TO-LISTEN-YOU-A-LUSTFUL-AND-PROMISCUOS-WOMAN-HE-IS-NOT-GOING-TO-HELP-YOU-SO-I-CAN-DO-ANYTHING-I-WANT-WITH-YOU-JUST-WAIT-AND-YOU-WILL-FEEL-SOMETHING-QUITE-PLEASING-!", the horrible voice screeched.

What happened next was something Lisa hadn't even once seen in her darkest nightmares. The demon stretched out the blobs on its back; they burst open and a black tentacle came out from each of them. There were at least 10 of these protruding out of the monster's back. When Lisa saw this, she was paralyzed with fear. Then the demon aimed the tentacles at her and released them; these black, slithering cords began to whip and strike her with great strength all over her body. They also tore off her clothes, leaving Lisa totally naked. As the demon saw Lisa in her natural beauty, it became very horny. So the tentacles grabbed Lisa by her arms and legs, lifting her up in the air. The monster brought her chotch closer to its face. Then it sticked out its long red tongue and began to lick her all over; the slimy organ licked Lisa's face, then her boobs and nipples, then her stomach and finally her pussy. She was screaming with horror and disgust.

After the beast had finished licking her, it raped her in the most diabolical way. It used its tongue to rape her pussy, one of the tentacles to rape her butthole and another one to rape her mouth. This gave the demon real pleasure – and real suffering to Lisa. The pain she felt when the demon raped her was excruciating; it was like her whole body was set on fire. When the demon finally came in her butt and in her mouth, she felt like dying; the demonic cum was burning her mouth and butthole like an acid. Her pussy was a wreck; the demon had used its sharp tongue to rub every inch of it – leaving the whole thing as it had been wiped with sand paper. Tears were flowing from Lisa's eyes, demon cum out of her mouth and butthole – and demon saliva mixed with blood out of her pussy. Lisa felt herself to be a filty and disgusting slut.

When the demon was finally done with her, it let her arms and legs loose from the tentacles. She dropped down and landed on her feet. When Lisa saw the beast had let her go, she didn't hesitate to escape; she wanted to get away from the monster that just raped her. So she began to run as fast as she could. So Lisa ran through the great zodiac constellations and finally she ended up at the Andromeda galaxy. This sight gave her such an awe the fear had to make room for it. She stopped and looked at this galaxy with amazement: the stars were circling its centre just like the bubbles in a jacuzzi – in fact, it was of the same size! This sight relaxed and soothed her mind. Lisa wanted to dive into that pool of stars – and she did! This stellar bath gave her such a pleasant feeling of both body and soul she could no longer remember the horrible violation the demon had done to her. When she got out of the pool of stars, her hair and body had become glorious; an innumerable amount of stars were attached to her skin and hair all over! She was still naked, but she didn't feel ashamed. It was like she was clothed by the starlight!

Then something horrible happened: the demonic arm suddenly appeared from the middle of the galaxy! It reached out and began to grope all around – trying to get Lisa! At first she was able to dodge the arm, but then its claws struck her left arm. Right after this the arm reached upwards and tried to crush her like a gnat. But she made a drastic leap and was just able to dodge the deadly blow. Lisa had reached a safe distance to the galaxy; the demon hand was still groping around, but now it was unable to reach her any longer. Soon it stopped moving and the arm was pulled back to the center of the galaxy.

Lisa was nervously anticipating what was going to happen next. She then saw how the galaxy began to swirl like a bubble bath. Even more and more bursts came from it – and then it happened: the demon leaped out of the galaxy with its full strength and landed just before her! The beast gave out a dreadful howl and tried to grab her. In the face of this horror Lisa was overcome with terror and she gave out a cry of fear. Then something wonderful occurred: her body – clothed with stars – suddenly began to shine with a blazing light! It hit the demon's eyes and they went totally blind. The monster covered its face and gave out an ear-piercing screech; it was in a horrible pain with its eyes completely fried. But then the demon went in a raging fury and was craving for vengeance. It let out all its wrath by unleashing its tentacles in every direction. Lisa tried to avoid them, but it was too late: one them got hold of her leg and she fell down. When the beast felt her like this, it directed all the other tentacles to her; they took hold of her arms, legs, waist, neck and hair, holding Lisa perfectly still. The demon laughed in a victorious manner and got its jaws fully opened. It began to walk towards her in a slow and steady manner. Lisa was schocked as she saw the terrible maw of the beast: it was big enough to swallow her up whole! She could smell the stench of 10 000 rotten corpses coming out of it! The demon was done with raping her flesh; now it wanted to devour it and add it to the collection! This would be the end of her!

Lisa saw how hopeless her condition seemed to be. In her despair and terror she made one last attempt to pray God for help. So she bowed her head and said this:

"My God, I confess before you all the sins I have done against your law. I have broken your command "Do not commit adultery" so many times with my boyfriend. Forgive us, Father, for all the wicked things we have done. I believe you can help us if its your good will. My Lord, save us and we will dedicate our lives to you! Amen!"

It was then Lisa saw a bright light which began to shine above her. She lifted up her sight and saw the constellation of Orion, the great hunter, above her. Lisa saw one specific part of it – Orion's sword – shining with glorious light. And then, suddenly, an awe-inspiring thing happened: the bands of Orion got loosened and the bright, shining sword fell down from the sky – right next to Lisa!

The brightness of the sword went down quickly. Now Lisa was able to see what was next to her: a shining sword with a glowing blade! In an instant she turned her head and saw a horrible thing: the demon had reached so near its jaws were able to capture her – just like a flytrap catches a frog! The upper jaw began to shake and was just about to close. But then Lisa took hold of the sword's handle with her right hand. She pulled the sword and then struck the blade to the roof of the beast's mouth. Just then the upper jaw began to close and Lisa pulled herself out of the maw; she barely got out when the jaws got clashed together.

For quite a while Lisa was lying still and didn't dare to look before her; she was overcome by fear, stress and anxiety – filling her body from top to bottom. Being still she tried to take heart and look what was before her, but failing many times. Finally Lisa was able to open her eyes and look before her – with her heart pounding and her mind filled with fear for the worst.

Finally Lisa saw the demon lying before her: it was upon its belly, with its jaws tightly closed and its wings down collapsed. The sharp top of Orion's sword had gone through the monster's head and was now visible between its horns. The demon was lying there lifeless and it seemed to be mortally wounded. But suddenly its head began to move. Lisa got scared and pulled herself even further – for the tentacles were now without life. Between the demon's teeth a growl could be heard. It's eyes were bleeding, burned and totally blind. And then the horrible sound of coughing and glorping was heard. The demon opened its jaws so its tongue came out. Then Lisa's ear was able to hear the same demonic voice as before. But it was no longer fearsome and powerful: now it was weak and full of sorrow. Its message, however, was as chilling as before. The words she could hear were thus:

"YOU-HAVE-NOT-WON-CHAOS-CANNOT-BE-DESTROYED-!"

After these words there was a deadly silence. Then the blade of Orion's sword began to shine brightly like before. The light spread itself from the sword all over the demon's body, filling it from the inside out. And then there were light-filled cracks appearing all over the body. Finally these cracks covered the body from top to bottom. Then – all of a sudden – the demon exploded into a pure, blazing light. Lisa lost her conciousness.

9. Awakening

"*Wake up, Liz! Are you okay?*", a voice was speaking.

Lisa was already recovering from the blazing light that had knocked her unconcious. Her eyelids were closed tight so she was unable to see who was speking to her. But as she was listening more closely the voice began to sound very familiar. Lisa was trying to open her eyes, but that wasn't easy; her eyelids felt so heavy as if they were made of lead. So her eyes were opening very slowly and she was able to see in small steps. At first Lisa saw it was a young man speaking to her. And soon she was able to see who it was: her beloved David!

He was sitting next to her, kneeling and leaning over her face. Lisa was lying on the floor. But she got up, embraced David, kissed him and wept greatly for her joy. She had received her beloved back and the nightmare was over! She look him in the eyes and saw they were bright as a pair of sapphires; there was no trace of the darkness where the demon had lurked – at least she knew it was so. But Lisa knew nobody would believe her story, and that's why she decided to keep it all to herself.

Lisa was embracing David for quite a while and was unwilling to let go. But then he spoke to her:

"Hey! Loosen up a bit! Will you, Liz?"

When Lisa heard this, she let go and stood up. Now she was able to look around her: she saw they were back at the hospital – in the very room where her journey to the dark abyss had begun. After looking and wondering for a while she spoke to her boyfriend:

"Can you remember what happened?"

"I remember we were watching some stars at your place. And then there was this weird, bright light, and ...and ... and that's all I remember." David responded.

"And how do you feel now?", asked Lisa.

"Not very bad but not very good, either. There is some bad feeling inside me.", he said nervously.

Lisa was uneasy upon hearing this; could there still be something dark inside him? But soon there was an unexpected turn of events: David burst into tears and he embraced Lisa with strength. She was surprised to see him like this, since he had never wept before. After a little while she asked him:

"What's the matter? Why are you crying?"

"I'm so sorry for everything!", David sobbed.

"What are you talking about?"

"It just came back to me. Before the bright light came, I was full of evil thoughts towards you. And that's not all: for a few months I have been filled with lust and desire for your body. The more time we spent in bed, the more lustful I became. Finally it consumed me so that all I saw in you was a way to satisfy my desire. But now I feel different; it's like all that evil lust and desire inside me has disappeared! Now I see you

as the dear and sweet Liz I fell in love. Can you ever forgive me?"

"I already have forgiven you, just like God has forgiven both of us!"

"Do you think we can have a brand new start for our relationship and life together?"

"I think we can, with God's help!"

At the very moment the door was opened. Lisa's parents and the doctor saw both of them embracing each other. When the others saw them, they were amazed how David was now cured. But they were happy and decided not to disturb the young couple. So the door was closed.

10. The New Beginning

After these events Lisa and David went back to the farm with her parents. From now on their vacation went on in peace – with no more evil disturbance. The young couple decided to retain from sexual relations as long as they spent time at the countryside. They found this time to be quite refreshing; they could focus more on spending time together and to learn more about each other's thoughts, feelings and interests. David wanted to talk more about God and religion – something they had never talked to one another! These discussions led to an interesting end: David found faith in God and Jesus – and felt it was just the piece missing from his life! He had tried to fill the empty spot with pleasures, but now it was really filled!

All this gave Lisa even deeper and stronger faith in God and Jesus. She and David decided to save sex for their upcoming marriage. Studying the stars was for Lisa just as dear as before – and David got interested in it, too! However, her encounter with the sinister demon had left a permanent mark in her soul. But Lisa had fought at the side of the light and she had won her beloved David back from the dark side – both body and soul!

So they went on with their lives.

"Canst thou bind the sweet influences of Pleiades, or loose the bands of Orion?"
Job 38:31

"Put on the whole armour of God, that ye may be able to stand against the wiles of the devil.
For we wrestle not against flesh and blood, but against principalities, against powers, against the rulers of the darkness of this world, against spiritual wickedness in high places."
Ephesians 6:11–12